Heinemann
New Windmills

Out of the Darkness

Born on the same day thousands of miles apart, Liam is unwanted and unloved; Leila is loved and cherished. But their futures are linked. Pursued by evil killers, Leila turns to Liam for help. As they try to escape, Liam begins to realise that their fates are inextricably connected. But why would anyone want to kill this gentle and loving girl? Liam tries to understand but as the moment of destiny rushes closer, is he prepared for the truth?

About the Author

Nigel Hinton was born in London in 1941. As a child he was much more interested in reading, rock music and films than he was in school.

After leaving school Nigel had a number of jobs before deciding to train to be a teacher, which, 'to my complete surprise, I discovered that I loved'.

Nigel had been teaching for nine years when he wrote his first book, *Collision Course*. He originally wrote the book to read to his class but was encouraged to get it published by his pupils. After its publication, Nigel gave up teaching so that he could spend more time acting and writing. Since then he has written many successful titles, including the best-selling *Buddy* trilogy.

Other titles by Nigel Hinton in New Windmills:

Getting Free
Buddy
Buddy's Song

NIGEL HINTON

OUT OF THE DARKNESS

Lancashire Children's Book Award Winner

Heinemann
New Windmills

Heinemann Educational Publishers
Halley Court, Jordan Hill, Oxford OX2 8EJ
A division of Reed Educational and Professional Publishing Ltd

OXFORD MELBOURNE AUCKLAND
JOHANNESBURG BLANTYRE GABORONE
IBADAN PORTSMOUTH (NH) USA CHICAGO

Text © Nigel Hinton 1998
First published by Penguin Books Ltd 1998
The moral right of the author has been asserted
First published in the New Windmill Series 2000

04 03 02 01 00
10 9 8 7 6 5 4 3 2 1

ISBN 0 435 12500 1

Cover illustration by Kevin Jenkins
Cover design by The Point
Typeset by 🔺 Tek-Art, Croydon, Surrey
Printed and bound in the United Kingdom by Clays Ltd, St Ives plc

This book is dedicated to
Ella Price and Dylan Beattie

I would also like to thank the following people
who gave me advice and truly helped to make
this book possible:

Lorraine Beasley and her class at
Bushey Meads School, Bushey, Herts:
Marvin Barretto, Sarah Bell, Hayley Brockwitz,
Gavin Brown, James Burgess, Tom Carlton, Peter Cates,
Helen Cole, Louise Davies, Kelly Edwards,
Peter Fletcher, Samantha Gough, Amy Jones,
Scott Kilbane, Christine Kirkham, Kelly Landells,
Louise McLeod, Claire Nickless, Rebecca Paine,
Manisha Pandya, James Rose, Emilie Simson,
Emma Tannian, David Taylor-Hone, Jill Tear,
Jill Westbrook, Clare Youens.

Bill Allison and his class at
Hodgson High School, Poulton-Le-Fylde, Lancs:
Stuart Armer, Steven Brook, Jackie Bullough,
Darren Burnell, Nichola Carter, Emily Clapham,
Ben Coombs, Laura Creighton, Stewart Deaville,
Amy Duckworth, Nicholas Dunn, Kimberley Edge,
Andrew Fletcher, Erica Greenhalgh, Chris Hargreaves,
Dane Kelly, Paul Lonsdale, Clare Magee,
Lindsay Parker, Luke Pattison, Helen Poole,
Cheryl Robinson, Laura Rowe, Corinne Sanderson,
Clare Sponder, Emma Toole, Jonathon Waterhouse,
Chris Watkinson, Andrew Whitham.

Chapter One

**3.30 p.m. Tuesday 28 April,
Stoke-on-Trent, England**

'This child doesn't want to be born,' the white-haired doctor said, smiling down at the woman.

He felt sorry for her. It had been a long, painful labour. What a pity that this last delivery of his forty-year career should be so difficult.

'Come on, my dear, just one more effort and we'll drag the blighter out whether he likes it or not.'

3.35 p.m.

The doctor held the boy's ankles as he finally slid out into the world. He cleared the baby's mouth then slapped his tiny buttocks.

Liam took a large gasp of air and began to howl.

The doctor cut and tied the cord then handed him to the mother. She was sweating and exhausted. The pain had been more terrible than she'd ever expected and her mind was filled with one thought, 'Never again.'

She looked at the top of the baby's head and she didn't like him.

From the first, Liam was a difficult child. He fed little and cried a lot. His parents worried about his slow weight gain, and the sleepless nights began to wear them out.

They both said later that it was the birth of Liam that started the breakdown of their marriage.

8.45 p.m. Tuesday 28 April,
Shimla, India

In a small palace on the outskirts of town, where the hills began to rise towards the high peaks of the Himalayas, Leila was born.

She lay calmly sleeping in her mother's arms for a few minutes then her father picked her up and carried her towards the open window.

He held her aloft towards the blue-black sky where one star shone huge and bright directly above, then he cradled her in his arms again.

'Poor child,' he whispered low, so that her mother would not hear. 'What a fate awaits you.'

Then he turned and walked towards the door. Outside in the ante-room, the twelve people, who had flown in from all over the world for this moment, stood and waited their turn to kiss the infant's feet.

Chapter Two

The nurse looked at Liam's arm.

It was probably broken. There were bruises on the side of his face. And, strangely, bruises on the inside of his legs.

'He fell down the stairs, you say?' she asked the mother.

'That's right. Ask him if you want,' the mother said.

The nurse looked at Liam.

'Poor you,' she said, smiling. 'Fell down the stairs, did you?'

Liam glanced at his mother then nodded.

He was a good-looking little boy, the nurse noted. He was a bit thin and had rather dark rings under his eyes but he had a beautiful face. And there was no trace of tears. Unusual for a four-year-old. He must be in a lot of pain but he was determined not to show it.

'We'll have to take him down to X-ray for his arm,' the nurse said.

She hoped that the mother would stay in the waiting area so she could have a chance to chat to the boy in private and ask him a few questions.

'I want to be with him,' the mother said quickly.

And she stayed with the boy all the time – through the X-ray and through the setting and plastering of the arm. She never once held the boy's hand or spoke a comforting word to him but she never left his side.

The nurse noticed that when the pain was at its worst the little boy looked at his mother. That was all. He never cried, he never groaned or flinched. He just looked at his mother.

And that look.

'It was like a dog looking at its master,' she said to a colleague later that evening. 'No, really, just like a dog.'

She wrote a short report about the incident and it got passed on to a Child Welfare Officer. A file was opened, pending further developments.

Two days before the plaster came off Liam's arm, his father left home.

Liam liked his dad. He was funny and he gave him cuddles. But he wasn't around the house very much. His job took him away for weeks at a time. So Liam was used to him not being there. He knew his dad had left, though, because his mum told him.

'Gone and good riddance,' she said. 'He's not going to treat me like that. She's welcome to him. What did he ever give me, except you?'

Liam didn't really understand what she was talking about but he picked up the bitterness in her voice. And he understood 'Gone', and he couldn't forget 'Good riddance'. For years, whenever he heard someone say the word 'Gone' he automatically added to himself '. . . and good riddance.'

His dad stayed gone and good riddance for nearly a year then he turned up unexpectedly and took Liam out to the seaside for the day. They ate fish and chips on the beach. His dad built a sandcastle and they bought a small flag on a stick to put on the top of it. Liam went on some rides on his own. Then they both went on the Ghost Train and he screamed when he saw the skeleton and his dad laughed and held him tight.

His dad said that they would go out together every month and they did. For a whole year, from the age of five-and-a-half to six-and-a-half, Liam saw his dad every fourth Saturday. Then he stopped coming.

Gone, again. And good riddance.

Liam had a card from him for his seventh birthday. It said 'Lots and lots of love from Dad' but that was the last time Liam ever heard from him.

Gone. And good riddance. For ever.

Liam hid the card in an old jigsaw-puzzle box but he told his mum that he'd torn it up because he knew she would be pleased. Sometimes he took the card out and looked at it. Sometimes he even kissed the words.

Chapter Three

Leila grew up surrounded by love.

For the first five years of her life she was hardly ever out of her mother's sight. There were seven servants in the palace but it was the mother who fed and changed and bathed the baby. It was she who played with her, talked to her, smiled at her and crooned songs to her. She who held out her arms to her as she took her first steps. She who showed her pictures and read her stories. She who walked with her in the walled garden and pointed out the birds and the flowers.

Leila's father saw her each day for an hour in his study before she went to bed. He was a tall, dignified man. The rest of the world found him aloof and severe but then they never saw him with his beloved daughter. They never saw the smile of delight whenever she came into his room. They never saw the tenderness in his large dark eyes when he held her in his arms and danced round the study. They never heard his laughter as he crawled across the floor with her on his back.

Her parents always spoke English to her and she learned to speak it, like them, with no trace of an Indian accent. Then, at the age of six, a man came from Argentina and began teaching her Spanish and French. He taught her to read and write and gave her lessons in Maths and Astronomy. In the evenings she often lay on the grass in the garden gazing up through a telescope while her tutor and her father told her legends about the stars and their influence on the Earth.

It was also at the age of six that her father began taking her into town on Friday evenings. He left her there every weekend with one of the palace servants who lived with her large family in a two-roomed apartment just off the market square. The servant adored Leila, and her seven children quickly grew to love her too.

After the calm and space of the palace, the little apartment was crowded and noisy. But Leila liked the rough and tumble of the children. She liked the chatter and the laughter as she sat with them in a circle on the floor and shared their meals. She liked their darting games in the busy alleyways.

From them she learned how to charm the traders in the market into giving them leftover vegetables and fruit at the end of the day. With the other girls she went to the river and washed their clothes, pounding them on the rocks and dipping them into the icy waters from the mountains. The oldest boy, who at thirteen was the head of the family now that his father was dead, taught her how to scavenge for scrap metal which he hammered into shape – rough beakers or small pans – and sold in the market.

At night she slept with the children on a carpet in the corner of the small bedroom. As they all lay there in a tired tangle, the sound of their breathing comforted her and she never missed the softness of her bed at home.

By chance, Leila's seventh birthday fell on a Friday. The children of the servant were invited to the palace for the little party.

Leila's father realized that the children might be overawed by the interior of the palace so he set a table in the garden. Even so, they stood around shyly for nearly ten minutes until a loud cry from a peacock made them all jump. Then they started to laugh at their fright and soon they were running and playing with Leila.

They were hungry when they sat down to eat. Indeed, their mother had to give a fierce look to her oldest son when he snatched some bread and started eating at once. He immediately put the bread back minus one bite and hung his head in shame. Leila quickly offered the bread to him and her wide smile put him at ease.

After the meal there were more games in the garden until night fell and the children went home with their mother. Leila stayed with her parents for another hour then her father took her into town to stay with the family as usual. He parked the car near the market square and they strolled towards the apartment. The night was unseasonably hot and the square was filled with people hoping to catch the occasional breeze.

As Leila and her father got close to the building they could see the children and their mother sitting outside trying to keep cool. Leila had just noticed that the oldest boy was not with them when there was a bright flash and the building shook. Her father pushed her to the ground and covered her with his body as debris fell all round them. When they stood up again they saw the gaping hole in the apartment wall.

There was a moment of total silence as they looked at the building. Then came a terrible wail from the mother and Leila knew that the oldest boy had been in the apartment.

Her father plunged into the building and made his way upstairs through the rubble but there was nothing to be done. The boy was dead.

They took the family back to the palace with them. As they drove into the courtyard Leila's mother ran out from the door.

Her father got out of the car and Leila heard him say, 'It has started. They know she's here.'

The look of fear on her mother's face told Leila everything. The bomb had been meant for her.

Alone in her bed that night, Leila cried for the boy who had died because of her. The next day she boldly knocked on her father's study door and told him that he must take care of the servant's family now that the boy was dead. Her father held her close and told her that he had already arranged it.

The following night Leila and her parents left the palace. They drove into the mountains then abandoned the car and set out on foot, taking the high passes and staying in remote settlements until they were sure they were not being followed.

Chapter Four

Liam's favourite part of the day was from the end of school until his mother got home from work.

He liked walking home with Mrs Martin who came to pick up her daughter, Clare. She always saw him to the gate and then waited until he opened the front door, went inside, and waved to her from the front room to show that everything was all right.

Mrs Martin was nice. Sometimes on the way home she bought ice cream or a bar of chocolate for him and Clare. She always asked what sort of day he'd had at school and she listened when he told her. Once she asked him how he'd got a cut near his eyebrow. But he didn't tell her.

Then, when he got home, he liked the quiet of the empty house. No shouting. No banging. Just quiet.

He would turn on the TV and watch it with the sound off, curled up on a sofa with a cushion pulled close to his chest and his shoes off so that he didn't make a mark.

At half-past six he would go upstairs to his bedroom and wait. When he heard the front door close he knew what sort of mood his mother was in. If it closed with a gentle click he could go down. But if it banged very loudly then it was best to stay in his room, go to bed, and hope she didn't come up to see him.

Sometimes when there was a gentle click and he went down he would find her slumped in an armchair with her shoes off and her legs stretched out in front of her. That meant she was very tired. Liam liked those times because she let him rub her feet gently. She would close her eyes while he rubbed and a slight smile would come on to her lips. When she smiled like that he felt a big squeeze in his heart because it must mean that she loved him.

Three weeks after Liam's tenth birthday, he came home and found someone else rubbing his mother's feet.

He closed the front door and ran into the front room to wave to Mrs Martin. He saw his mother in the armchair and a man sitting on the floor in front of her but he didn't stop to look – he went straight to the window. He pulled the curtain aside and waved to Mrs Martin as he always did. She waved back and turned away.

Liam kept watching her. He didn't want to look back into the room. He stared and stared out of the window as Mrs Martin and Clare walked away.

Then his mother said, 'Well, aren't you going to say hello?'

Still he stared out of the window.

'Liam?'

He shook his head and stared out of the window.

'Liam . . .'

The tone of her voice had changed to the one that scared him most of all and he didn't dare keep looking out of the window.

He turned.

He tried not to see but he couldn't help it.

His mother was in the armchair. Her legs were stretched out. Her shoes were off and the man was sitting on the floor holding one of her feet. His thumbs were moving, round and round, on the fleshy part of her foot, just below the toes.

'This is Mr Watling,' she said. 'He works with me. You know – I've told you about him. Say hello.'

Liam walked towards the man.

'Stevie, meet my son, Liam,' his mother said.

'Hello,' Mr Watling said to Liam, letting go of his mother's foot and holding out his hand to shake.

11

Liam got closer and closer. He could feel his eyes opened wide and he could feel his breath going in and coming out.

Then Liam threw himself head-first at the man.

His small fists pounded on to the man's chest and face.

Liam felt his mother pulling at his neck and he felt the man struggling to stand up but still he thrashed with his fists. Then his fists started to hit air. He opened his eyes.

Mr Watling was standing in front of him looking amazed. Blood was starting to trickle from his nose.

Liam wanted to laugh but his mother whipped her arm round his neck, grabbed a handful of hair with her free hand and began jerking his head backwards and forwards. His teeth rattled but he didn't care. Mr Watling was still in reach. He leaned back against his mother, raised both feet, and kicked Mr Watling full in the crutch.

His mother shouted something and began to slap his head. The blows crashed against his ear. He struggled to try to twist away from her but her arm tightened round his neck. He raised his hands and grabbed hold of her face, digging his nails into her skin. His mother screamed as he pulled downwards and scratched her cheeks.

Then Mr Watling loomed up from where he had been crouching, gasping for air. Mr Watling bunched his fist and swung it straight into Liam's belly.

The breath shot out of Liam's lungs and he hung, limp, from his mother's neck-hold. Mr Watling stepped forward and punched him again in the belly.

His mother let go of him and Liam fell to the floor.

Liam's mother said it was his fault that the Social Services got involved. She said he must have told his teacher.

It wasn't true. He had tried to hide the bruises when he was changing for PE but the teacher had seen them anyway. He had asked lots of questions but Liam hadn't said anything. And he didn't say anything to Mrs Cooper, the Case Worker who came to the house. His mother knew he couldn't have said anything to Mrs Cooper because she was always there for the interviews but she still blamed him for what happened.

'It's your fault,' she said. 'You've gone mouthing off so it serves you right.'

He clung on to his mother's legs and begged her to let him stay with her.

'Too late now, isn't it!' she said. 'They've made up their minds.'

'I don't want to live with Gran. I want to live with you. Please, Mum. Please let me live with you. I'll be good – I promise!'

'You're lucky they're not sending you to a home. You'd change your tune there, I can tell you.'

Then Mrs Cooper came to collect him to take him to his gran's house. Suddenly his mother held on to him as if she didn't want him to go. She squeezed him and kissed him and looked upset and promised she'd come to see him.

His gran's house was only thirty miles away but his mother never came. At first he told himself it was because his mother and Gran didn't get along, but then he heard that she was getting married. She was still his mother – nothing could ever change that, his gran said – but now she was going to be called Mrs Watling.

Then he knew. He would never be able to change her mind and make her love him. There was someone else in the house with her now. There was someone else to rub her feet when she was tired. She didn't need him for anything.

Chapter Five

Leila and her parents lived for a year in Afghanistan in a remote monastery that was built into the side of a mountain. Deep in the interior of the rock was a large eight-sided room known as the Power Centre and it was there that Leila spent her days. She studied Arabic and worked with a group of young monks weaving intricate designs into a huge carpet.

When the time came to move on, Leila had her hair cropped short and, dressed as a boy, she set out with her father. Her mother left separately and went back to India while Leila and her father went south to Pakistan. They flew from Karachi to Jakarta and then took a fishing boat along the coast of Indonesia before crossing the Timor Sea to Australia.

They spent six months with a professor of Physics in Perth and another six months going walkabout in the outback with a group of aborigines. The leader of the aboriginal group was an old man whom the others called 'The Big Man'.

The Big Man had lived all his life in the Gibson Desert. He couldn't read or write but he knew more than anyone else about Dreamtime and the legends of the spiritual beings who guide the world. The Big Man and Leila never spoke about The Dreaming. But the old man and the young girl often sat staring at each other across the flickering light of the campfire and their silence was full of meaning.

One day some of the aborigines reported seeing three strangers in the area. They were equipped for kangaroo hunting, said one of the aborigines, but they didn't act like kangaroo hunters. They were only pretending. The word 'pretending' alerted Leila's father. That night he and Leila said farewell to The Big Man and left the group, heading west towards the Indian Ocean.

For a year and a half, until she was eleven, Leila and her father lived in various countries in Africa. Some of their hosts were rich and powerful people living in cities, others were simple peasants whose homes were mere shacks.

The people they stayed with always welcomed them but it was a difficult life for Leila. She missed her mother and she missed her friends. The strain never showed, though. Everyone who met her was struck by her serenity, her strength and her sense of humour. She laughed easily and people laughed with her because they felt happy and light in her company. Her hosts knew they would respect her but they were always surprised by the way she won their hearts.

Her father saw the love she inspired and he knew exactly what these people felt. He had tried to think of himself just as a guardian of this special child but the loveliness of her qualities had filled his heart too. He had tried to tell himself that all parents had to let go of their children eventually but sometimes, looking at her smiling face, he had to fight back his tears.

He understood and accepted The Necessity but it still hurt.

Chapter Six

Liam kept telling himself that he ought to be happy now that he was living with his gran. Not that he was unhappy. His gran was kind to him – she fed him, washed his clothes and tried to make him feel welcome – but he knew that she was only looking after him because she felt she had to.

'I'm too old for this bringing up kids lark,' she said one day when she was particularly tired.

She got tired easily. She had something the matter with her heart and Liam knew she worried about it. She had to take pills and she was always asking Liam if she had taken them or not. At first he never knew but soon he made a point of noticing so that he could tell her. And he also made a point of not making her tired.

Noise made her tired, so he kept quiet. Making a mess of his room made her tired, so he kept it very tidy. Washing made her tired, so he wore his clothes until they were really dirty. He knew that any trouble at school would make her very tired, so he was always on his best behaviour.

He didn't like school much. When he went to live with Gran he had to join a new primary school. He went into the top year group. Everybody knew each other well because they had been together for years, so he felt left out.

Even at secondary school most people stuck with old friends. He felt lonely, but he never told Gran because he didn't want her to worry. Mostly he stayed quiet and tried not to get noticed. He found that he could do the school work easily and he liked doing it but he tried not to be too good in case people noticed him and picked on him.

His gran bought him a computer for his thirteenth birthday.

'One of my insurance policies has just paid out so there's some cash to spare,' she said. 'I know all you young people like these computer games and things nowadays. Waste of time if you ask me. Still, it'll keep you quiet, stuck in your room, I suppose.'

Liam did stay in his room but he didn't play games. Instead, he began surfing the Internet. He loved reading all the messages that people sent out to each other. Some of them were so strange. And some of them were so lonely. He could hardly believe how some people poured out their hearts to strangers. He never wrote anything himself.

He knew it was really silly but, whenever he turned on the computer and went peeping into other people's hearts and minds, he always hoped to find a special message for him. He knew exactly what it would say. *'Liam – I love you. I want you to come home but it's difficult. I know you understand. Mum.'*

Every evening, without fail, he told himself it was mad to hope to find this message. It was impossible and he knew it. But every evening, without fail, part of him believed he would find it. And at the end of every session, when he hadn't found it, he laughed at himself and told himself that it served him right for being so stupid.

But he didn't stop being stupid. It got worse. He started doing strange little things to make the message happen. He had to wash his hands before he turned the computer on and then he had to hold his breath all the way from the bathroom until he was sitting down in front of the screen.

And the superstitions didn't stop there. He was thirteen – an unlucky number, people said – and he was scared that something terrible might happen. To make sure he was safe he had to get out of bed the same side every morning. He had to dress the same way – starting with his socks and finishing with his trousers. And, most important of all, he had to make sure that he was never the first or the last person to leave a classroom.

It was stupid and he hated doing it but he was terrified to break the rules he had made. Just while he was thirteen – he told himself – he'd only do them while he was thirteen. Then he would stop. He promised God he would stop then, just as long as God made sure nothing terrible happened.

When he went back to school after the summer holidays everything started to be great. The teachers had decided to put him in a different class because his exam results had been so good. On the very first morning in the new class he sat next to Paul and they started talking straight away. By the end of the fourth week he knew that he had a real friend. Paul liked everything he liked and it was so easy to talk to him. They even supported the same football team.

It was Paul who persuaded him to try out for the Under-14s' school football team. Liam had never dared before but he loved the training sessions and he knew that he stood a good chance of being picked with Paul.

It was raining the lunchtime that Paul came running into the classroom just before the bell went for afternoon school. Paul's hair was plastered with rain but there was a huge smile on his face.

'We've done it! We're in the team,' he shouted.

The classroom was emptying as people made their way to their first lesson. Liam knew he ought to go now – to make sure he wasn't the last out.

'Mr Hume's just put up the list!' Paul went on.

'Great!' Liam said, smiling and feeling a burst of happiness in his chest. But he couldn't help noting that the room was nearly empty. Better move now.

He took a step towards the door but Paul grabbed hold of his arm.

'Hey, wait for me – I've got to get my things.'

Liam's heart was beginning to race but he stayed. Paul was his friend.

The room was empty now, apart from the two of them. That was OK – he'd just make sure that he went out of the door before Paul. No problem.

'Come on, we'll be late,' he said, watching Paul stuffing some books into his bag.

'No chance,' Paul said, closing his bag. 'I'm never late. Watch!'

And Paul barged past him and dashed out of the room.

Liam stood there, alone in the room. He felt his heart lurch and then knock loudly in his chest. The blood rushed to his face and he could feel the cool of the air against his skin.

Tears welled up in his eyes but he forced himself to walk to the door and out of the classroom.

Nothing terrible happened.

His teachers kept on being pleased with his work and Gran was delighted when he showed her his books and the good marks. Paul was still his friend. They both played well for the football team and got picked for every game.

But three months later he walked into the house and found Gran sitting so still in her chair. It was dark but even before he put the light on and saw her open mouth and the way her head was slumped to one side he knew she was dead. And the first thing he thought of was the day he had been the last one out of the classroom.

Chapter Seven

Liam ran upstairs to his bedroom. He didn't want to see Gran dead.

He sat at his desk and switched on his computer.

He stared at the screen for ages and then ran a search on the word 'Dead'. Dozens of sites came up with names like Dead Singers. Dead Parrots Club. The Grateful Dead. The one that he selected was The Dead Room.

For a long time it seemed as if there wasn't anybody there. Then a message appeared: *Hi! This is Nick. I live in Omaha, Nebraska. My wife died last week. I feel as if I'm burning up with pain. Anybody there?*

The message stayed there for a long time. Nobody replied and Nick didn't write anything more. Then Liam typed: *Liam. My gran is dead. What do I do?*

Immediately Nick started typing back: *Hi, Liam. I know how you feel. Do you want to talk about it?*

Liam shook his head at the screen and exited The Dead Room.

He lay on his bed and pulled the covers round him. He dozed for a while then he woke and made up his mind. He took a blanket off his bed and went downstairs. He went into the living-room and turned his head away so that he couldn't really see Gran as he moved towards her. Then he threw the blanket over her head.

He sat on the sofa and looked at her. The blanket covered her head and body but he could see her legs. They looked so cold and stiff. She was wearing her fluffy blue slippers which, she said, always kept her feet so cosy. Not now. Her feet must be cold.

At the thought of her cold feet, tears suddenly began to slide down Liam's face. On and on they poured, so hot down his cheeks and on to his chin before they dripped on to his sweater.

He wasn't crying for himself. He was crying for Gran. Everything about her life suddenly seemed pathetic. Her fluffy blue slippers. The pills she took for her heart. Her favourite TV programmes. The picture of Grandad she kept by the side of her bed. What a little life. And now it was over.

Still crying, Liam got up and went over to her. He took the blanket off her and looked down at her. It wasn't horrible at all. It was just sad. So sad. Her glasses were crooked. Her mouth was open. The lines on her face were so deep.

Her little life was finished. He wouldn't be able to talk to her again. He wouldn't see her pleased again when he told her how well he was doing at school.

He felt his legs give way and he crumpled to the floor and sobbed. He needed her but she had been taken away from him.

When he finally stopped crying, the carpet under his face was damp. He stood up and went to the sofa. The heating had gone off and it was getting cold. He put the blanket round himself and sat with his knees tucked up to his chin.

He stayed all night looking at Gran and he came to some conclusions. He had helped to kill Gran because of his stupid game. God didn't exist. Life was silly and small and meaningless and he hated it.

At nine o'clock the following morning he put the blanket over Gran again and rang Mrs Cooper, his Case Worker.

Mrs Cooper arranged for him to be put into 'Beeches Hall.' She kept saying, 'It's just a halfway house for a few days.'

There were twenty other young people in Beeches Hall but he didn't speak to any of them – not once. A couple of the boys threatened to beat him up if he didn't talk but he kept silent and they didn't carry out the threat.

He still kept going to school and he didn't say anything to Paul about what had happened. When they came out of school at the end of the day he still walked part of the way home with Paul as if he was going back to Gran's. Then, when they split up at the usual place, he doubled back in the other direction to Beeches Hall.

He was there for four weeks then Mrs Cooper came and told him that she'd arranged for him to go and live with his mum and Mr Watling.

'Only if you want to, Liam. It's up to you. It's your life. I want what's best for you. I can find you a nice foster home if you want to. But your mum's prepared to have you. There have been a lot of changes since you were there. She's married Mr Watling, of course. And there's the new baby – well, she's nearly three now. But, in a funny way, she might make it easier for you. Sort of take the pressure off. What do you think?'

Liam told her he didn't care. And he didn't. He had tried to stop feeling anything and it was working. The only person he liked was Paul.

Mrs Cooper said they'd give living with his mum a try. She made the arrangements and she came to Beeches Hall to pick him up.

Liam thought of sending a letter to Paul to explain, but he didn't.

Chapter Eight

Mr Watling told Liam that he should call him Stevie.

'You might even get round to calling me "Dad" one day, who knows,' he added.

Liam didn't call him anything. He simply didn't use a name when he talked to him, which wasn't very often. He was always polite, though – very polite. He knew Mr Watling hated his cold politeness and he knew it upset his mother.

'You're an ungrateful little . . .' she hissed at him one evening when they were alone in the kitchen. 'Stevie goes out of his way and you just throw it back in his face.'

Liam just looked at her and didn't say anything.

'God, you're a . . .' she shouted and grabbed hold of his upper arm and pulled and squeezed until it hurt badly.

He still just looked at her and she finally stopped hurting him and turned away to do the washing-up. He went up to his room and rolled up his sleeve.

There were marks on his arm where she had squeezed him. He stroked the skin where her fingers had been.

The move back to his mother's house – he never allowed himself to think of it as his home – meant that he changed school again. He had tried hard at his other school because he knew it pleased Gran but now he didn't care. Within a month he was in trouble for not handing in work on time. His Group Tutor sent a letter home.

Mr Watling came upstairs to his bedroom and stood there shouting and waving the letter. Liam didn't even look at him. He just stared at his computer screen.

Mr Watling called to his mother and she came up and they both shouted at him. Liam still stared at the computer.

Then his mother bent down and pulled the plug out of the wall. Liam swore at her and she swung the flex and hit him across the face with the plug. The back of the plug smashed on to his nose and made him bleed. He looked at the blood that splashed on to his hand, then he stood up. He was only going to walk out of the room but his mother stepped back as if she was scared and swung the flex again.

This time the plug hit him across the side of the head above his ear and one of the pins cut him open. He made to grab the flex and Mr Watling punched him twice. The first punch caught him in the belly and, as he doubled up, the second punch hit his chin and knocked him out.

When he woke up he was lying on his bed and Mr Watling was carrying his computer out of the room. Liam hurt too much to do anything but lie there and watch.

Mr Watling installed the computer in the little boxroom that he called his study. Liam asked his mother to let him have it back in his bedroom but she refused.

'You don't deserve it,' she said. 'And anyway it'll be useful for Stevie.'

Mr Watling was useless with computers. He kept asking for help but Liam just stood silently in the study doorway and watched him making mistakes. He laughed when Mr Watling finally crashed a whole programme. Mr Watling jumped up and came towards him but Liam grabbed the broom that was next to the door.

They looked at each other for a long time and then Mr Watling turned back to the computer.

Every day for two weeks Liam asked his mother to let him have his computer back. She kept saying no. One day when he got home from school, Liam went out to the garage and took a hammer out of the toolbox.

He went into the study and stood looking at the computer. The hammer was so heavy. He let it swing gently by his side, feeling its weight rocking his arm backwards and forwards.

Then he lifted the hammer and smashed it into the computer screen.

He felt sick and sad when he looked at what he had done. The computer was his last link with Gran and Paul and all that other life. Then he started swinging the hammer again at the rest of the equipment – the keyboard, the speakers, the mouse, everything. The whole system was ruined. Mr Watling would never be able to use it again.

His mother came into the study as he stood looking at the mess. She screamed at him and then slapped him round the face. He didn't flinch. She slapped him again. Again he stood and let her do it. Then she grabbed a handful of his hair and jerked and jerked his head. He could feel the hair tearing away from his scalp.

And now he started to cry, but not because of the pain. It was the things she was saying.

'I hate you!' she screamed. 'I hate you and I wish you were dead! Why don't you die? Why don't you die?'

Chapter Nine

Leila and her father left Africa and crossed the Atlantic on an old cargo ship. They arrived in Brazil and then travelled south, following the Paraná River.

Leila became more and more excited because she knew her mother was waiting for them in Argentina. In a small, cheap hotel on the border she rushed into her mother's arms and held on to her tightly. Her mother kept saying how grown up she looked and Leila knew it was true. Two-and-a-half years had gone by. She was eleven.

Leila lay on the bed holding her mother's hand. There were no panes in the windows of the hotel and moths and mosquitoes found their way in through the slats of the shutters.They danced round and round the tall glass of the oil lamp. Some flew down into the lamp and met a fiery death. In the silence, Leila could hear the sudden crackles as they died.

The next day the family travelled on, following the Paraná. Four days later they crossed the river and headed west towards the Andes.

Their contacts had arranged for them to move into a huge ranch on the edge of the plains near the mountains. Leila loved looking at the snow-topped peaks in the distance – they reminded her of home.

The nearest school was over fifty miles away but Leila had a number of tutors who came, usually for a month at a time, to keep up her studies.

There was still plenty of free time though, and Leila spent most of it riding. She loved horses and she quickly became an excellent rider. Her father told her that there was no danger for the moment so she spent hours alone, galloping on the vast open plain or following the winding paths up through the forests of the foothills.

A year after the family arrived at the ranch there was an important international conference in Argentina. Among the hundreds of delegates were the twelve people who had visited Leila on the day she was born. At the end of the conference these twelve people made their way separately and by roundabout routes to the ranch. They stayed for a week.

It was during this time that Leila began to learn of her role in the Design.

Chapter Ten

The only thing that made life bearable for Liam at his mother's house was his little half-sister, Danielle. She took to him from the first moment she saw him. She called him 'Miam' and she always wanted to be with him. He spent hours having to play all sorts of babyish things but he didn't mind. She was so sweet and he loved it when she put her arms round his neck and kissed him.

His mother got annoyed when she saw them together.

'It's not normal – a boy your age and a little baby like that,' she said one day.

But every time she tried to stop them playing a game together Danielle screamed and made such a fuss that she had to give in.

Liam bought Danielle a cuddly koala bear for her third birthday. It was only a small toy – he couldn't afford anything bigger – but she wouldn't let go of it all day.

'What are you going to call him?' Liam asked.

'Miam,' Danielle said.

'That's my name,' Liam laughed.

'It's his name too and I love him.'

She took the koala to bed with her and she held on to it even at mealtimes. Mr Watling had bought Danielle a huge doll and Liam could see that he hated the fact that she preferred the little koala.

Then, a week later, the koala disappeared. Danielle took it to bed with her and the next morning it was gone.

'It can't just disappear! Somebody must've taken it,' Liam said.

'Don't be stupid,' his mother said. 'Who'd steal a stupid toy?'

Liam looked across at Mr Watling and Mr Watling looked back at him. Neither of them said anything.

'Well, I'll buy her another one,' Liam went on.

'She's got enough toys as it is,' his mother said.

'I want to – she loved that koala.'

'You're not to buy her one, and that's it!' his mother snapped.

Liam knew she meant it.

Danielle kept asking him where Miam was.

'I'm here!' he kept joking.

'No, baby Miam!' Danielle insisted.

'He must've gone back to his mummy,' Liam said.

He went to the shop to look at the toy koalas but he didn't dare buy one.

One day his mother asked him to look after Danielle while she went out. Liam felt proud and pleased because it meant she trusted him, and you only trusted people you loved.

He sat on the floor and played 'families' with Danielle. It was her favourite game. He had to get all her dolls and cuddly toys and dress them and make them go shopping and have something to eat and then go to bed and then get up and start all over again.

Liam was feeling so happy that he even tried to bring Mr Watling's big doll into the game but Danielle said it was nasty and made it stay on the sofa.

After a couple of hours Liam had to go upstairs to the toilet. He was only gone about a minute but as he started down the stairs there was a scream and then Danielle started crying. When he rushed into the room she was lying on the floor next to the table. She had climbed up on to a chair and fallen and banged her face against the table leg. Blood was pouring from a cut under her eye.

He picked her up and ran upstairs to the bathroom. He got a clean towel and wet it and pressed it against the cut. Danielle screamed and howled and wriggled and tried to get away. Liam tried to keep the towel pressed against her but she was moving so much he was scared it would rip the cut open more. He took the towel away and Danielle stood there sobbing while blood and tears dripped on to the floor.

Liam took her into his arms and carried her downstairs – he would have to go to the hospital. Just as he got to the front door it opened and his mother was there. She took one look at Danielle and grabbed her from him. Her eyes flashed hatred at him then she was gone, running down the street.

Liam closed the door and slumped down on the stairs. He was still sitting there two hours later when they came back.

'Six stitches because of you,' his mother snarled.

She went into the living-room. Liam followed her in. She sat on the sofa with Danielle cradled in her arms. He knelt down and reached out to stroke the little girl's hair.

'Don't you touch her!' his mother shouted.

He stayed there, crouching in front of them, staring at the floor.

'Oh, get out of here!' his mother said.

He went upstairs to his room and lay face down on the bed.

Some time later his door banged open. He glanced up to see Mr Watling moving towards him. He had a belt in his hand.

Liam covered his head with his arms and pressed his face down into the pillow. He just lay there and let Mr Watling hit him. The belt whipped down across his back five times.

Long after Mr Watling had gone, Liam finally got up and gently took his shirt off. His back was still red with the flat strap of the belt but the worst thing was the bruising round the ribs where the buckle had crashed against his side.

He looked at the welts and bruises and he made a vow. He would never let Mr Watling do it again. He was fourteen now. Next time . . .

Liam knew it was only a matter of time. He couldn't go on living with them.

His mother almost never spoke to him and she had forbidden him to play with Danielle. The little girl still tried to climb up on his knee sometimes but he had to gently push her away and say, 'No, Danielle – Miam's busy.'

He could hardly bear to be in the same room as Mr Watling, especially at mealtimes. Mr Watling made horrible noises when he was eating. Just looking at the way he chewed his food made Liam feel sick.

Every night while he was waiting for sleep to come, Liam thought about the same thing. The world was going to be destroyed but there was a special spaceship that only he knew about. He would get on it and only two other people could come with him – Danielle and Paul. They would fly off into space just before the world exploded and they would cruise and cruise across the darkness until they came to a planet where there was air and water and everything they needed. They lived there and it was all new and fresh and they were happy together.

School broke up for the summer. On the first day of the holidays his mother cooked egg and chips for the evening meal. He tried not to listen to the slapping noises that Mr Watling was making but when he saw a bit of egg yolk trickle off a chip on to his stubby chin, Liam felt sick.

He put down his knife and fork and pushed his plate away. His mother told him to get on with his meal but he shook his head and stood up.

'You sit down and eat or you'll be sorry!' his mother yelled.

'I can't. He makes me sick. Look at him!' Liam said, pointing at the blob of yellow on Mr Watling's chin.

He started towards the door but Mr Watling jumped up and grabbed him. Liam jerked his arm free and then landed a punch right on Mr Watling's cheekbone. Mr Watling staggered back and fell over the edge of the sofa.

Liam ran up to his room, locked the door and pushed the chest of drawers hard up against it. His mother and Mr Watling banged on the door and there were a couple of thumps as someone threw their shoulder against it, trying to burst it open. Then there was silence.

Liam slept for a while then early the next morning he packed some clothes into a shoulder bag. He opened his door very quietly, tiptoed down the stairs, and left the house.

His gran had left him a bit of money in her will and he waited until the bank was open and took most of it out. He had more than enough to afford trains or buses but he didn't want to buy a ticket in case anyone remembered him and told the police where he'd gone. So he walked instead.

He took minor roads and tracks where there was the least chance of being seen. He slept in barns and huts. One night he couldn't find anywhere and he had to sleep in the woods. Luckily it was a warm night but he was scared by the noises in the darkness.

The biggest risk was buying food but he always waited until there were a lot of other customers in the shop. Then he kept his head down and bought the things quickly. And he made sure that he found a public toilet every day so that he could wash. People would notice him if he was dirty and looked as if he was living rough.

Two weeks later he arrived in Derby and allowed himself to take a bus. Even so he didn't want to be seen alone so he offered to carry an old lady's suitcase and got on the bus with her so that people would think they were together.

She got off at Nottingham and he followed her. He stood in the bus station as the bus pulled out and that was where he first saw The Rat.

Chapter Eleven

Leila lived in Argentina until she was thirteen. It was a time of peace and she was happy.

Then late one night she and her parents packed hurriedly and left. Her father had received a warning telephone call and they had to go into hiding again.

They travelled north across the plains and jungles and mountains of South America until they arrived in Venezuela. They stayed there a couple of weeks and then caught a flight to Los Angeles.

Her father had friends all across the United States and they spent nearly a year travelling from one safe house to another, trying to shake off the people they knew were searching for them.

The longest time they stayed in one place was eight weeks in Sweetwater in Texas but, even there, word came that their enemies were closing in so they moved on. From there, they drove across country to Atlanta.

Leila's father rang a contact in England and put Leila on to the first available flight. She was on her own.

Her parents flew to New York and then on towards India.

As they sat on their plane heading back to their homeland, each of them was lost in thought. The mother held on to a scarf that Leila had bought for her at Atlanta airport. The father closed his eyes and tried to keep a picture of his beloved daughter in his mind. They prayed that it might not be true but they both knew it was possible that they had seen Leila for the last time.

Chapter Twelve

Nobody knew his name. Everyone called him The Rat, even himself. He never used the words 'I' or 'Me'. He said things like: 'The Rat's hungry,' or 'Listen to The Rat, he knows what he's doing.'

Liam listened to The Rat because it was true – he *did* know what he was doing. He was only sixteen but he'd been on the streets since he'd run away from a residential care centre at the age of ten.

'Lots of bad things have happened to The Rat,' he told Liam one day, 'but that place was the worst.'

He didn't look anything like a rat. He was good-looking, with sandy hair and green eyes, and he tried to keep himself as clean and tidy as possible. The only thing rat-like about him was the quickness of his movements and the way his eyes were constantly on the move, looking for danger.

He knew every CCTV camera in town and he knew just the right moment to duck his head or turn aside so that he wasn't seen.

'The Rat doesn't need TV stardom,' he said, 'he's a real-life star!'

When Liam left home he'd imagined that he would have to sleep in cardboard boxes but The Rat had his own house. True, the windows were boarded up and there was no furniture but it was reasonably clean and there was running water. It didn't belong to The Rat, of course, but he'd even had keys made – the council had nailed and padlocked the front door but somebody had forgotten to do the back door. He gave a key to Liam.

They slept together on the one mattress in the house. On the first night Liam had lain on the edge of it, trying to keep as far away as possible so that they wouldn't touch.

'What's your problem?' The Rat had said, reaching out and dragging him closer. 'The Rat's not gay. And he doesn't care if you are or not. We're a team – The Rat and The Brat. And there's no sex in this team.'

And with that, The Rat had put his arm round Liam and hugged him. Tears had rolled silently out of Liam's eyes. The Rat's arm had stayed round him until they had fallen asleep. And from then on the same warm, protecting arm held on to him every night.

'How have you managed for six years?' Liam asked him once. 'You know – for money and stuff?'

'You name it, The Rat's done it.'

'Murder?' Liam joked.

'Not yet,' The Rat said, and there wasn't a laugh in his voice.

'Would you?' Liam asked, his heart knocking in his chest.

'Not for money,' The Rat said. 'But The Rat might have to protect himself one day . . . or pay someone back . . .'

Most of the time they got their money from being 'runners'. The Rat had contacts all over town and they often needed someone to deliver things to another part of town. Sometimes it was just a message, mostly it was small packages.

'Money, credit cards, passports, drugs – all sorts,' The Rat said when Liam asked what was in them.

The Rat also sold information. Being on the streets meant that he knew everything that was happening. Certain people were sure to slip him some money on being told, for example, that there was a new plainclothes policeman in town, or that the vice squad had got a different unmarked car, or that some shopkeeper always took his day's takings to the bank at three-thirty. The Rat taught Liam how to keep his eyes and ears open.

When there was no money to be got from 'running', they stole stuff from cars or houses. The Rat didn't like stealing – 'Too much risk, too little return. It's for losers.'

The big-time losers, in The Rat's opinion, were the young people who ended up on the 'Meat Rack', waiting around the city centre for a car to cruise by and pick them up.

'They've all got habits to support,' he said. 'Crack, smack – they gotta have it, so they do that. Never get a habit, Brat. The Rat knows – he's been there.'

In one spectacular week they made so much money from 'running' that The Rat decided they were going on holiday. They caught a bus to Blackpool and hired a caravan. The weather was hot and sunny and they lazed around at the caravan park or the beach during the day and spent the evenings at the funfair. They met different girls every night and spent lots of money to impress them.

After two weeks they were broke and headed back to Nottingham.

A couple of days later they were doing a delivery of a small packet to one of their regular calls, a man called Trev. The Rat rang the bell and the door was opened by a man they'd never seen before.

'Run!' shouted The Rat.

Liam spun round and dashed towards the front gate. Out of the corner of his eye he saw The Rat veer off and jump the low wall into the next garden. Liam kept heading towards the gate then a man stepped out from behind the hedge and blocked his way.

Liam turned to follow The Rat but ran straight into the man from the house. Hands grabbed him and he was pushed to the ground. He was turned over on to his stomach, a foot was planted in the middle of his back and both arms were twisted up towards his shoulders. He tried to struggle but his arms were jerked so painfully that he groaned in agony and lay still.

He stayed there listening to the shouts and the sound of running feet then a car screamed to a stop on the street. He was lifted to his feet and he saw the police car parked at the kerb.

Chapter Thirteen

Liam waited in the police car for about ten minutes then one of the other policemen came back.

'The other one's gone,' the man said, still panting from the chase.

They drove him to the police station and locked him in a room. He sat down at a table and waited. An hour later a big, red-faced man came into the room followed by a policewoman. The woman stood near the door while the man came and sat down opposite him. He said his name was Inspector Dean and that the woman was PC Mason. He switched on a tape recorder and quietly began asking him questions – What was his name? Where did he live? What was in the packet? Who was the other boy?

He told him his name was Liam, that he'd been sleeping rough, that he didn't know what was in the packet, and that he had met the boy on the street and didn't know his name.

Inspector Dean wrote the answers down on a piece of paper then he got up and left the room followed by PC Mason. Half an hour later Dean came back in. He was alone and his mood had changed. He banged the door behind him, leaned over the table, and started shouting the questions again. This time the tape recorder was not running.

Liam stared at the man's huge hands pressing on the table. Wiry, black hair spread down from his arms and across his wrists. There were even tufts of hair on his thick fingers. Liam concentrated on looking at the hands and gave him the same answers as before.

The man's hands bunched up into fists and he pounded the table.

'Don't lie to me!' the Inspector roared. 'You've got no idea what I can do to you!'

A chair scraped and the Inspector sat down opposite him. There was a long, long silence and Liam felt a trickle of sweat run down his side.

'There were drugs in that packet,' the Inspector said at last, his voice quiet again. 'You're in big, big trouble, lad. You won't even give me your address or surname so there's no one I can call to come and help you. No one knows you're here and I can do what I like. Right? Now I want some answers.'

Liam shook his head. How could they know what was in the packet? The Rat had got away. The man was bluffing. All he had to do was keep quiet and not tell him anything.

It seemed such an easy thing to do, to stick to the same answers he had already given. But he hadn't bargained for Inspector Dean. There was something really frightening about him – his size, the sudden changes in mood, and, above all, the way he could go on and on endlessly asking the same questions. And if Liam altered a single word of what he had said before, the Inspector was on it in a flash and the questions would start all over again.

Bit by bit, Liam became exhausted. All he wanted was for the questions to stop. His hands started to tremble and he felt sick.

Three hours after the questioning began, tears suddenly filled his eyes. He ducked his head and tried to blink them away. The Inspector leaned across the table and roughly lifted Liam's chin up so that he couldn't hide the tears.

'Come on, little boy – we're nearly there. Nearly there. All I want is answers.'

The Inspector kept Liam's face held up and just stared at him. Liam felt the tears pour out of his eyes and then a sob shook him.

'There, there, lad,' the Inspector said gently. 'Just a name or two, that's all it is – and then you can rest.'

Liam nearly broke. Sobs were beginning to rock his whole body and he could feel snot trickling from his nose and mixing with his tears. He almost gave The Rat's address; almost said the name of his mother and where she lived. But at the last minute he held on and blurted out another name.

'Mrs Cooper!'

'Who?'

'Mrs Cooper. Stoke eight-nine-zero-seven-six-three.'

'Your mother?'

'My case worker.'

'Yes,' Inspector Dean said, with a slight smile, 'that figures. Well, it's a start, Liam. It's a start. I'll go and get PC Mason and we can get your answers down on tape. Make it official, eh?'

He let go of Liam's chin and stood up and left the room.

Liam brushed the tears off his face and sniffed hard. He wouldn't break. He would never tell Dean about The Rat and where he lived.

He lifted the skin on the back of his left hand with the nails of his right thumb and forefinger. He pinched and rubbed until the nails broke the skin and he began to bleed.

Dean would never break him.

He went on pinching and rubbing until he wanted to cry out with the pain.

But he didn't cry out.

And he would never betray The Rat.

Chapter Fourteen

As soon as she came into the room, Liam could see that Mrs Cooper was worried. And when he told her how long it was since he'd left home, her mouth opened in shock.

'But your mother didn't . . .' Mrs Cooper began and then stopped. She put her hand up and pinched the top of her nose as if she had a bad headache.

Liam suddenly realized. His mother hadn't even bothered to report that he was missing.

There was a stab of hurt in his heart. Then he turned the pain away. It was finished. He would never let her hurt him again. He hated her.

Then he looked at Mrs Cooper. Her forehead was all wrinkled up with worry lines. And he knew why. She hadn't even known he had run away. She was in trouble. And now, in the new coldness of his heart, he realized something else – he could help her or he could make things worse for her. He had power.

She was easier to fool than Inspector Dean and Liam made her believe his whole story. She insisted on being there for the next interview at the police station and she took his side, saying that there was simply no evidence that he had done anything wrong. Dean knew he had lost and he let him go.

Then Mrs Cooper started talking about the future. Liam told her about the fights at home. The worry lines came back to her forehead and he knew why – it was her job to prevent things like that. He said he just wanted to forget all about the beatings from Mr Watling, as long as he never had to go back home. Mrs Cooper agreed with him.

He said he wanted her to contact his father and she promised to try. In the meantime he had to go back to Beeches Hall until something could be sorted out.

Some of the same boys were still at Beeches Hall but no one threatened to beat him up this time. He knew there was a look in his eyes that scared them. And he liked that look. He liked the hardness he could feel in himself. He didn't care about people any more.

Even when Mrs Cooper told him that his father had refused to meet him, he was proud of how his heart felt nothing.

His mother and father were nothing to him. They were strangers. He was alone, but he didn't care.

'Just get me out of this place,' he said to Mrs Cooper when she started to say how sorry she was about his father.

Mrs Cooper was stupid. She was soft. She could be worked on.

The warden at Beeches Hall said that while he was staying there he had to go back to the same school he had been at before. On the very first day his old friend Paul came up and tried to talk to him but Liam punched him. It wasn't a hard punch but it was enough to stop Paul from trying again.

Liam was in Beeches Hall for three weeks then Mrs Cooper came and told him she had found something special for him. One of her ex-colleagues was working for another authority south of London.

'He's worked out that it's cheaper to send people to proper boarding schools than it is to keep them in places like Beeches Hall. He's set up a sort of experiment with a pretty exclusive sort of private school down there and he's looking for a bright boy to send there to see if it can work . . . It's up to you, of course, and I don't mind if –'

'Yes,' Liam said.

'I want you to think about it . . .'

'I don't need to think about it. I want to go.'

Mrs Cooper suddenly looked unsure and Liam knew he had to be more careful.

'Please, Mrs Cooper,' he said, putting on a sad voice, 'it'll be like a new start for me.'

That's all it took – a phoney sad voice – and she was on his side again.

'That's exactly what I hope,' she said. 'And I want you to take that chance, Liam. I'm going out on a limb here.'

'I won't let you down, Mrs Cooper – I promise. And I'll never forget what you've done.'

She smiled and squeezed his hand.

A week later she drove him down south. They met up with her colleague, Gwyn Phillips, and the three of them went to Frazergate School.

It was an enormous old ironstone house set in acres of woods and fields. The huge entrance hall was wood-panelled and it smelled of polish. The headmaster, Mr Roach, and his wife came down a wide, carpeted staircase to welcome him and then took him up to show him his room. It too was carpeted and had a wash basin and a shower in the corner. The lattice windows looked out over a small lake.

Liam stood and listened to Phillips and Roach going on and on about what a wonderful chance it was for him but he could see through all their fancy talk. All Phillips cared about was his precious 'experiment'. As for Roach, he kept going on about 'financial benefits all round' and it was obvious that the only thing that interested him was the money.

'Well?' Mrs Cooper said, beaming at him as she stood outside ready to go.

'It's great,' Liam said.

She suddenly grasped him into her arms and gave him a hug. Her breasts felt soft and squidgy against his chest and he wanted to laugh. Then she let go of him and quickly got into her car and drove off.

'Right – I'll leave you to settle in,' Mr Phillips said. 'Remember, this is an important experiment I'm running. If it succeeds, it could be adopted nationwide and I could . . . Anyway, I'm going out on a limb here and I'm relying on you to make it work. By the way – I like my clients to call me Gwyn. OK?'

'Yes . . . Gwyn,' Liam said, smiling a big friendly smile.

He stood and watched as his new Case Worker drove away.

From upstairs in the school Leila watched Liam as he waited until the car was out of sight then stuck his middle finger up in the air. He turned and looked at the imposing building. For a moment an anxious look crossed his face but then he breathed deeply, raised his shoulders, and walked proudly towards the door.

Leila nodded and smiled to herself. He was the one.

Chapter Fifteen

There were only thirty-five pupils in Frazergate School. Six of them lived locally and went home in the evening but the rest were boarders. Most of these came from abroad and were, Liam soon found out, incredibly rich.

All the other pupils had their own cars – usually the latest model BMW for the girls, and powerful sports cars for the boys. One boy from Saudi Arabia even had a Ferrari.

They nearly all had their own flats in London and most of them left for the weekend at midday on Friday and didn't get back until midday on Monday. Sometimes they even flew out of the country for the weekend. One of the girls was from New York and she celebrated her birthday by taking some of her friends there for what she called a '3C Weekend – Concorde, Champagne and Cocaine'.

Despite the cars and designer clothes and expensive lifestyle, it soon became obvious to Liam that most of them were at Frazergate because of some problem or other.

A few were there for their own protection. One boy from the Philippines had killed a seven-year-old girl in a car accident and had been sent to England to avoid prison. The parents of Shireen, a girl from Lebanon, had put her in the school to try and keep her away from the terrorist group she had joined in her own country. A boy from Colombia was there because his parents were scared that he was the target for kidnappers at home.

Most of the others, though, were there simply because their parents didn't want them around. They all openly talked about how their parents hated them or how they hated their parents. They had nearly all been through some kind of therapy and they joked about how they were 'S-U', screwed-up.

Behind all the jokes, Liam knew how much they hurt. They hadn't found a way to stop the pain like he had. They were soft and stupid because deep down they still hoped that things would work out. They still cared.

A sixteen-year-old Belgian boy wet his bed every night. Three of the girls and two of the boys had tried to commit suicide in the past and proudly showed the scars on their wrists to prove it. A lot of them were on tranquillizers. Most of them drank heavily. All of them got depressed easily and were liable to go on wrecking sprees.

In the first month that Liam was at the school, four table tennis tables were smashed, two TVs were kicked in, the pool table was set on fire and the baize of the snooker table was deliberately ripped. They were all quickly replaced. Nobody was punished for these things and the pupils just laughed and said that Mr Roach liked it when things got damaged because he always charged double the real price when he added the cost to their fees at the end of term.

When Liam arrived at the school, the other pupils tried to get him to talk about himself but he found it easy to freeze them out and they soon left him alone. He knew they called him 'The Spook' but he didn't care. The only one who interested him was Leila.

On his first evening at the school she had come up to him and said, 'Hello, my name's Leila. I've been looking forward to meeting you.'

He had been so surprised that he hadn't even asked her what she'd meant.

She was not like anybody else in the school. She too went up to London at the weekend but she stayed with a guardian and didn't go clubbing and drinking like everybody else. She was quiet. She was clever. She worked hard. She always handed in her work on time and, invariably, got the best marks in every subject. She didn't smoke or swear or gossip or flirt.

Everything about her seemed guaranteed to make the others hate her and yet they didn't. On the contrary, they liked her and went to her with their problems even though she was younger than they were. There was something calm and strong about her that they wanted to be near.

Liam never went to her or started a conversation with her but he liked it whenever she came and sat next to him. He didn't let it show, of course, and he even tried to freeze her out like he did with the others but it didn't seem to work with her. She just sat down and talked to him as if they were old friends. She never said anything special but life always seemed better after she had spoken to him.

There were only three classes in the school. Two of them were for the foreign students who were learning English, so Liam was put in the other group. This was supposed to be the exam class and, apart from Leila, the people in it were three or four years older than him.

Although she was only fourteen, Leila came top in all the work. The others were lazy and hopeless and, almost without trying, even Liam got better marks than they did. Then, bit by bit, he started trying and was surprised at how quickly and easily he learned, and how much he enjoyed it. Mr Roach said he was so pleased with his progress that he would enter him for some exams the following summer.

Gwyn Phillips was pleased with him too. He visited the school every week to see how things were going. Liam smiled and was polite and called him Gwyn and then gave him the finger as he drove away.

A week before the end of term, Liam was in his bedroom when there was a knock on his door. He was surprised because no one ever came to see him – he'd made sure of that. He opened the door and found Leila there.

'Yeah?' he said.

His voice was hard and unwelcoming but there was a kind of confused shiver inside him as he realized that part of him wanted to smile and ask her in.

'You're staying here over Christmas, aren't you?' Leila said.

He nodded. To make the maximum money out of the school, Mr Roach ran revision courses for pupils from other schools at holiday times. Gwyn Phillips had offered to find him a temporary foster home but Liam preferred to stay.

'Have you decided which courses to take?' Leila asked.

He shook his head.

'Your French needs improving and they're running a beginners' Spanish course. It's always useful to have another language,' Leila said, then she turned and walked off down the stairs.

Liam was stunned for a moment then he shouted, 'Get lost!' and slammed the door.

That night he dreamed of Leila.

He could see her very clearly – her smooth light-brown skin, her large brown eyes, her straight eyebrows, her long, graceful neck, and the black glossy hair swept back from her oval face into a long plait. She was sitting at her desk. She smiled at him and then went back to writing in a book. In his dream he found himself moving closer to look at the book. Over and over, she had written in capital letters the words SPANISH and FRENCH.

On the first day of the holiday course, Mr Roach asked Liam which classes he would like to go to. He had been going to say Maths and Computer Studies but at the last moment he asked if there was room in the French and Spanish classes.

Liam worked hard and he was amazed at the progress he made. The teacher lent him some tapes and he spent most of his free time doing extra work.

Every evening when he finished work he went out for an hour's run before going into the gym to work out. He didn't know why, but he suddenly felt that he wanted to get fit, really fit.

Two cards arrived for him on Christmas Eve. They were from his case workers, Mrs Cooper and Gwyn Phillips. They wished him a Merry Christmas and a Happy New Year and they both signed 'Love'. He tore them up, threw them in the waste-paper basket, and looked out of the window.

A bitter cold wind was blowing outside and it was beginning to sleet. Most people would be indoors getting ready for Christmas. He put on shorts and a thin T-shirt and went out for a long run.

Chapter Sixteen

Liam kept the training up during the Easter term. He pushed himself harder and harder every day and he took pleasure in the pain that was toughening up his body.

Leila never asked him about the courses he had taken at Christmas but she got into the habit of saying something in Spanish whenever they passed each other. He always understood what she said but he just looked blankly at her as if he didn't know what she was talking about.

He couldn't hide the improvement he'd made in French, though. When he got his first piece of work back with full marks he looked up and saw her smiling at him. And it wasn't just French: week by week throughout the term his marks got better and better in all his subjects.

Gwyn Phillips arranged for Liam to stay for the Easter Holiday Course. He decided to take French and Spanish again and, like last time, he expected to be the only one of the term-time students who would be staying. Then Leila had a phone call.

The students' phone was just down the stairs from Liam's room and he always ran down to answer when it rang. It was silly really, but he liked that moment just before he picked it up and there was still a chance that it might be for him. It never was, of course, but after he'd called the person to the phone, he would go upstairs and leave his door open so that he could overhear the conversation.

This time a man's voice asked for Leila. Liam called her and then went up to his room to listen.

'Hello,' he heard her say as she picked up the phone. There was a long pause, then she spoke again and her voice was tense. 'No, nothing . . . No, I would have noticed, really . . . I *am* careful . . . Look, I'll stay down here until you think it's safe . . . Don't worry . . . You take care as well . . . And promise you'll ring me . . . OK. Bye.'

Two days later Leila told him that she was staying for the Holiday Course. He was pleased but he didn't let it show.

Liam got into the fight just before the Easter weekend.

The boy, Michael Wilton, had picked on Liam since the first day of the Holiday Course but Liam had managed to keep his temper. Then, somehow, Michael had found out that Liam was in care. From then on there was an endless stream of comments and jokes. Liam took it and took it, and then snapped.

Michael was two years older, and taller than Liam, but just one punch laid him out.

As Liam looked down at the boy sprawled on the floor, he felt a surge of pride. He wanted to raise his arms in the air and dance over his opponent. All his training had paid off – he was fit and strong and nobody could touch him. But his joy only lasted a moment.

One of the girls looked at Michael lying there unconscious and went rushing off for help.

By the time Mr Roach got there, Michael had come round and was sitting on a chair but he was still too groggy to walk. Mr Roach fussed round him, getting him something to drink and telling him that he was all right and that there was no need to call a doctor. Then he screamed at Liam to go and wait for him in the library.

It was nearly three hours before Mr Roach arrived in the library.

'You stupid little idiot!' he shouted as he slammed the door. 'My God! I've just spent two hours persuading

Mr and Mrs Wilton not to sue me because of you. They wanted to call the police and have you arrested. I would have let them too – except I don't need the bad publicity, thank you very much. Do you realize what something like this can do to a school if it gets out? It could ruin us! Oh, I had my doubts about you from the very first – someone with your background mixing with my kind of pupils – but you seemed to be doing so well, keeping yourself to yourself, working hard. And now this!'

Mr Roach was in front of him, shouting in his face. Liam knew he ought to lower his head in shame and say he was sorry, but he couldn't. He *was* sorry and he really wanted to stay at the school but he stared directly in Mr Roach's eyes and didn't say anything.

'Your future here is hanging by a thread – do you know that? I've rung Mr Phillips but the damned office is closed for Easter already. Typical! In the meantime, if you so much as breathe out of turn you'll be back where you came from quicker than blink. Now get out of my sight.'

The school was empty over the Easter weekend. Even Mr and Mrs Roach went away for a short break, leaving Mrs Roach's aged parents to keep an eye on the school.

Liam and Leila, the only two pupils left, were told they could go down the road to the Little Chef and charge their meals to a special account which had been arranged for them. Liam made sure he didn't go at the same time as Leila and yet all the way through his meals he found himself hoping she would come in and sit with him.

On the Friday night, he dreamed about her. He saw her reading in a classroom. She turned and smiled at him, and the gentleness and warmth of her smile gripped his heart. He woke up and found that he had been crying in his sleep.

At just after six o'clock on the Saturday evening, he left his room and started down the stairs to go to the gym.

Leila was at the phone, dialling a number, so he tiptoed back to his room and waited for her to go. He was looking out of the window at the ducks swimming on the lake when there was a knock at his door. He stayed quiet, but a moment later the door opened and Leila came in.

'Liam,' she said, closing the door and leaning against it.

'Just leave me alone, will you!' he snapped and turned back to look out of the window.

'Liam – I'm in trouble.'

'*You're* in trouble,' he sneered, not turning to look at her.

He heard her cross the room towards him. She put her hand on his shoulder and pulled him round to face her.

'I mean, Liam,' she said, and her voice was urgent, forcing him to listen and believe her, 'I mean that my life is in danger and I need your help.'

Chapter Seventeen

They walked in silence towards the Little Chef and Leila looked anxiously at all the passing cars. The mood was catching. When one car slowed as it came towards them, even Liam felt a sudden surge of tension. The light of the setting sun was bouncing off the windscreen, making it impossible to see who was in the car. It went past and he couldn't help looking over his shoulder until it was out of sight.

They sat in a quiet corner of the Little Chef and Liam waited until the waitress brought their drinks before he asked Leila what was going on.

'Liam, I can't explain it all, not now. You've just got to believe me. I think something has happened to my guardian – I haven't heard from him for three days and when I've tried to ring him there's no answer.'

'So he's out doing something or he's gone away – so what?'

'Liam, please! He promised to stay in contact with me. All I want you to do is to come up to London with me and see what's happened.'

'London! Are you kidding? Roach is just dying for a reason to kick me out. Do you realize what'll happen if he does? I'm in care, right? They'll stick me straight in some stinking residential centre.'

'I know.'

'You don't know anything!'

'Liam, I know a lot more about you than you think. But most of all, I know that I need you.'

He was astonished by the way the words 'need you' seemed to burst inside his heart and he found his eyes suddenly filling with tears.

'Ask someone else,' he snapped and looked away so that she couldn't see him blink the tears away.

When he looked back she was shaking her head and gazing down at the table. Then she raised her eyes and looked straight at him. He wanted to look away but he couldn't.

'Why are you at Frazergate?' she asked.

'Because . . . I don't know . . . because my case worker got me in here.'

Leila nodded. 'And that's unusual, isn't it? And she only got you in because she knew someone working down here.'

'How do you know that? he asked, but she ignored him.

'And why did you get that particular case worker? You could have ended up with someone else who didn't have a friend down here, but you didn't. Then think of all the things that led to you being in care in the first place. Go on, think of them.'

Liam thought of them – Where did it start? Mum not liking him? Oh, how that thought could still rip his heart. Dad leaving? Mum getting a job where Mr Watling worked? Mum liking Mr Watling? The teacher seeing the bruises?

'There are so many things, aren't there, Liam?' she said. 'Take just one of them away and everything is changed. But they all happened. And they all led you here.'

There was a tightening in his chest and he had to take a deep breath.

'You're mad,' he said. 'Are you telling me that everything happened so that I would end up here?'

'Well, you didn't end up anywhere else.'

A shiver ran down his spine.

'Was it just chance that brought you here?' she went on. 'Or a chain of events that means something?'

'What about you, then?' he asked. 'You're here.'

'Yes, I'm here. Here, where I'm meant to be. With the person I'm meant to be with.'

He shivered again, and again his eyes began to water.

'Please Liam – come to London with me. Will you?'

His throat was too tight to speak. He simply nodded and, at last, he managed to drag his eyes away from hers.

Chapter Eighteen

Liam waited at the end of the school drive while Leila went into the building to get some things and call a taxi. She came back carrying a large bag.

'A few clothes, passport – just in case,' she explained. 'I went into your room and took a few things for you too. I hope you don't mind.'

'What? I'm going to London with you – that's all. Then I'm coming straight back.'

'I couldn't find your passport,' she said, as if she hadn't heard him.

'I haven't got a passport! What the hell's going on?' he said. 'I told you – '

At that moment the taxi drew up and Leila quickly opened the door and slid the bag on to the seat.

She was so damned sure of herself.

A wave of anger and confusion swirled inside him and he suddenly turned and walked away towards the school.

He heard the door slam and he stopped and looked back. Leila was sitting in the taxi. She was leaning forward with her face in her hands, looking so lonely. The driver revved the engine and started to pull away.

'Wait!' he yelled.

The taxi was still trying to ease out of the drive into the traffic when Liam opened the back door. He sat down next to Leila.

'Thanks,' she whispered.

The nearest station was four miles away and they rode in silence. Leila paid the taxi and bought the train tickets. Liam was glad to hear her ask for returns, and while they waited for the train, he checked the timetable. With any luck they could catch the last one back from London and nobody would even know they had been away from school.

As soon as they got to London they caught a tube to Sloane Square and began walking down King's Road. They hadn't gone very far when Leila stopped.

'It's the second road down there on the right. Number twenty-six,' she said and held out a key. 'I'll wait for you in that McDonald's over there.'

'You're not coming?'

'I can't, Liam. They know what I look like.'

'Who? Who knows what you look like? The cops?'

'No.'

'Who then? What's going on? You've got to tell me!'

She shook her head and Liam suddenly thought of the Lebanese girl, Shireen.

'Are you a terrorist or something?'

Leila roared with laughter and, for an instant, he felt his temper rise. Then he looked at her laughing face and he couldn't stop a laugh bubbling up from his chest.

'No, Liam – I'm not a terrorist,' she chuckled. 'I haven't done anything wrong, I promise you.'

'OK,' he said, taking the key from her. 'Number twenty-six, yes?'

The white shutters of number twenty-six were closed but Liam could see light spilling through the slats. Leila's guardian must be in. He'd ring the bell, find out that everything was fine, and they would be on the train back to Frazergate within an hour.

He walked up the steps. The name Dr Prior was engraved on a brass plate on the door. He rang the bell. Almost a minute went by, then he rang again. He looked along the road – there was no one in sight. He waited a full minute then put the key in the lock.

As soon as he was in the house he knew there was something wrong.

All the lights were on but there was total silence. A hatstand was lying on the floor and there was a single shoe on the bottom step of the stairs. The shoelace was still tied. The dark-green stair carpet had scuff marks on each step as if something had been dragged upstairs.

Liam quickly looked through the door into the living-room. Pages of a newspaper were scattered on the carpet and a broken wine glass lay next to a chair.

He glanced along the corridor towards the kitchen but he knew that wasn't the way. Whatever he had to find was upstairs.

He reached the top step and opened the first door. The bathroom. The light was on and everything looked normal.

The next door. A bedroom. Dark, apart from the yellow glow from the street lamp outside. He flicked the light switch but nothing happened. He moved on to the third door.

There was a bad smell outside the door but it didn't prepare him for the stench that hit him when he pushed it open. His stomach heaved and he swung round and threw up before he could get to the bathroom.

All he wanted to do was run outside and breathe fresh air but he knew he had to see what was in the room. He pulled up the front of his sweater until it covered his nose then he looked into the room.

The old man had been tied to the bed. He was naked apart from his boxer shorts and his throat had been cut. Blood had soaked into the sheets, dying them a raw, rusty red. But it was clear that he had been tortured before he had died. There were bruises and burn marks all over his body and face and one of his ears had been cut off.

Liam felt his stomach heave again. And this time he did run. Along the corridor. Down the stairs. Stumbling. Almost falling when he reached the bottom. Saving himself by crashing against the wall. Pulling the door open and standing on the top of the steps and dragging air into his lungs.

A huge shudder shook him and he jerked forward and was sick again.

He leaned against the metal railings, waiting for his head to stop spinning. He closed his eyes and then opened them again.

That was when he saw the black Audi parked across the road. The front doors swung open and two men got out. The driver was a short, fat man with a blond crew-cut and the man on the far side of the car had dark hair and brown skin.

They weren't policemen. And if they were the men who had done those terrible things to that old man . . .

Liam jumped down the steps and turned left but the driver dashed across the road and blocked his way. The brown-skinned man ran round the car and started across the road to block the other direction.

'Hey, listen . . .' Liam said, holding up his hands and moving towards the short, blond man as if all he wanted to do was explain. 'Listen, I don't want any trouble. Please.'

The man fell for the scared tone in Liam's voice. Liam saw him relax.

'Please,' he said again as he moved closer to the man.

A smile of victory began to lift the man's fat lips as he looked past Liam to the other man.

'It's all right, Nayeem,' he said in a mocking voice, 'he doesn't want any trouble.'

Liam didn't give any warning. He didn't bunch his fist or swing his arm. He just kept moving closer and then suddenly thrust his open hand forward and smashed the heel of his palm on to the man's nose.

The man staggered back in pain and Liam burst past him.

There was a cry from behind and Liam heard the other man break into a run.

'Get him, Nayeem! Get him!' the driver screamed in anger and pain.

Liam sprinted as fast as he could, grateful for all those hours of training he had done. After about a hundred metres he knew that Nayeem couldn't keep up. He glanced back and saw him standing in the road waiting for the car. The driver had got in and was starting it up.

Liam ran on, reached the end of the road and turned left. He sped along the pavement and then stopped. There was a house facing him at the end of the road – it was a dead end. He could hear the screech of tyres as the car skidded round the corner behind him. There was no way back.

He ran towards the house. There was a side gate on the left and he dashed towards it, praying that it wasn't locked. He flicked the latch and pushed. The gate crashed open and he ran through and along the side of the house just as he heard the car stop in the street outside.

He reached the back garden and his heart sank. There was a wall all the way round it. It was taller than he was and there were jagged shards of glass set into the concrete along the top. He looked back and saw the two men charging towards the side gate. He would have to get over the wall. He took a few steps backwards then ran and leaped.

He grasped the top of the wall and he felt the flesh of his left hand slice open on a sharp piece of glass. He clung on and hauled himself up. He swung his body up over the top and there was a stabbing pain in his knee as some glass ripped through his jeans. Then he rolled over and tried to straighten up as he dropped on the other side. He landed awkwardly and fell forward, gasping in pain as he put his weight on to his cut hand.

He was getting to his feet when he heard the men jump on the other side of the wall. There were yells of agony as their hands hit the glass and he heard them both crash backwards. One of them jumped again and Liam saw brown hands land straight on top of the glass spikes. Nayeem moaned and fell back, leaving blood running down the glass. They wouldn't try again.

Liam looked round. He was in a narrow alleyway. He turned left and ran. The alleyway opened out on to a street. Down to the left he could see the lights of King's Road and he ran towards them. Better to be on those crowded pavements than alone in these quiet streets.

His left hand was bleeding badly so he pulled some paper tissues from his pocket. He bundled them into a ball and forced himself to grip it tightly.

When he reached King's Road he crossed over and mingled with the crowds heading towards Sloane Square. There was no sign of the Audi or the two men as he passed the end of Dr Prior's road but he still waited for a couple of minutes at the side of the McDonald's to make sure.

Leila saw him as soon as he opened the door. She picked up the bag and hurried towards him.

'He's dead,' she said. It was a statement not a question and he knew she had been expecting it.

He nodded.

'There were two men outside . . .' he began but she pushed past him and went out of the door.

'We've got to get away from here,' she said as he caught up with her.

They crossed Sloane Square and went into the tube station.

As they stood on the platform waiting for the train, Liam looked anxiously at the stairs, expecting to see the two men suddenly appear. There was a rumble in the tunnel and a blast of air as the train arrived. They got in and it seemed ages before the doors slid together. Then, finally, they closed and the train jerked and moved off.

Only then did Liam slump down on the seat and relax.

Chapter Nineteen

When they came out of the tube station at Embankment they crossed the road and stood by the side of the River Thames. The wind was whipping across the water and Liam began to shiver as he told Leila what had happened at the house.

'You think they tortured him?' she asked when he finished.

'He was in a terrible mess,' he said, and another shiver shook him as he remembered Dr Prior's injuries. 'We're going to have to go to the cops.'

'We can't,' Leila said fiercely. 'It won't do any good. They'll never catch the people who did it – they're too clever.'

'What about Doctor Prior? We can't just leave him there.'

'He's dead. We can't do anything for him.'

Leila turned and looked at the river. Her face was calm and Liam felt another wave of anger rise up against her. Her guardian was dead and she didn't even care. She didn't care about anyone. She'd known it was dangerous to go near the house – that's why she'd sent him rather than go herself. She'd just used him. He could have been killed.

'I had to let you know what we're up against,' she said, turning and looking him straight in the eye.

'What?'

'You think I was scared of going into the house so I sent you instead. But it's not true.'

Liam caught his breath and his shivering stopped. How had she known what he was thinking?

'I was sure Doctor Prior was dead,' she went on. 'But I needed you to believe me. You saw what they did to him. That's what they want to do to me.'

'Why? Why the hell do they want to kill you?' he asked angrily, still finding it hard to believe.

Leila just shook her head and his anger burst.

'Why don't you tell me anything?' he shouted.

'Because there's a difference between wanting to know and needing to know,' she said calmly. 'I'm telling you what you need to know. There are people who want to kill me. People who killed my guardian and who'll kill you if they get hold of you.'

Liam felt a pain in his hand and realized that his fingers were digging into the cut on his left palm. He looked down and saw that he was bleeding again.

'And I'm telling you it's no good going to the police,' Leila went on. 'They'll think we've done it. Your fingerprints are all over the house and you've been in trouble with the law already. And when they finally realize we're innocent, they'll let us go and those people will know where to find us.'

Liam felt as if a trap was closing round him. He wanted to run. But where to? Back to Frazergate. But if Leila was telling the truth . . .

'I'm telling you the truth,' Leila said.

A shiver shot up the back of Liam's neck.

'If we go to the police or if we go back to Frazergate,' she continued, 'those people will find us. Anyway, Roach won't let you stay at the school – you know he won't. All he thinks about is money. As soon as the weekend's over he'll be on the phone to Gwyn Phillips and you'll be back in care.'

As she spoke the words, Liam knew it was true. He had been hoping against hope but, deep down, he knew his time at Frazergate was finished.

'Liam,' Leila took hold of his arm and gripped him tight, 'I want you to trust me.'

'Why?' he said, pulling his arm free. 'You got me into this mess. Why should I trust you?'

'It's a good question,' she said, looking at him steadily. 'Only you can answer it. I'll wait over in the tube station for the next ten minutes then I'm catching a train. If you want to walk away, I'll understand.'

He watched her cross the road then he turned and looked at the river. Lights were shaking and sliding on the dark water and he gazed at them.

Why should he trust her? She was caught up in something dangerous. She wouldn't tell him what was happening. He could get in trouble. He could even get killed.

And yet . . .

There was something about her. What? Impossible to say. He hardly knew her and yet somehow he felt he knew her really well. And she seemed to know him. She seemed almost able to read his thoughts. And she made him feel . . . What? Made him feel . . . that she needed him. That he mattered. That he counted.

Did he trust her?

Yes, he did. He couldn't say why – but he did.

He crossed the road and went into the tube station. She was standing by the ticket barrier.

'What are we going to do then?' he asked.

'We've got to get away from here. Out of the country.'

'Leila, I can't. I'm in care. The minute the school tells Phillips I've gone, the cops'll be looking for me.'

'That's why we need to get as far away as possible. I need to get to Morocco.'

'Morocco!' A sudden fear swept through him. He'd never been out of the country before and here she was talking about going to Africa.

'Not straight away. I've got contacts in Paris – we'll go there first. I've got enough money.'

Paris. Morocco. A tingle of excitement cut through his fear. They'd probably be caught and he'd be sent back to a home. But he was going to end up in a home anyway, so what did it matter where they caught him? At least this way he'd get to see some of the world.

'But I haven't got a passport – you know I haven't,' he said, half hoping that she would have to change her mind.

'We'll have to get you one,' she said. 'Any ideas?'

And as she asked the question, Liam felt that she knew the answer. Because the minute he'd mentioned the word passport he had suddenly thought of The Rat.

'Maybe,' he said. 'We'll have to go to Nottingham, though.'

'OK.'

She reached in her pocket and pulled out two tickets for the tube. She handed one to him and he realized that she had known all along that he would go with her. Just as she had known that he would think of somewhere to try and get a passport. She was one step ahead of him all the time.

It didn't make him angry, though. He couldn't help a smile creeping on to his lips. He looked at her and she smiled back. And he knew he had made the right decision.

Chapter Twenty

They missed the last bus to Nottingham and had to wait until nine o'clock the following morning for the next one. They spent the night in the bus station.

'Do you know that guy Nayeem and the other one – the fat, blond one?' he asked as they sat in the dirty waiting-room.

'No.'

'Why do they want to kill you then?'

'I don't know. They've been paid money or they've been brainwashed with lies. It doesn't matter. They're killing machines. They do what they're told.'

There was a long silence then all Liam's fears bubbled to the surface again.

'We can't do this,' he said, leaning forward and shaking his head at the stupidity of it all. 'We're just kids. We can't go running off to Morocco. It's mad.'

'Nobody knows what they can do until they have to,' Leila said, putting her hand on his shoulder.

Her hand gripped his shoulder tight and he felt her strength flowing into him. She was right. He remembered his gran telling him about his great-great-grandfather who had left his village in Poland when he was only ten. He was the oldest in his family and there wasn't enough food for all the children so he had walked two hundred miles to the sea and got work on a ship and sailed around the world for six years before settling in England. If his great-great-grandfather could do that at the age of ten surely he could do this.

He felt filled with excitement and he could have talked all night but Leila said she was tired. She curled up on one of the benches and went to sleep with her head on his lap. She looked so peaceful and for some reason he thought about Danielle. He wanted to stroke Leila's hair the way his little half-sister had loved him to do but he didn't dare.

Did Danielle still remember him? Probably not. Anyway, best not to think about it. Best not to care.

At about three-thirty in the morning, the door to the waiting-room swung open and a policeman came in. Liam shifted his leg to warn Leila and she opened her eyes.

She looked across at the policeman then closed her eyes again.

'It's all right,' she said softly. 'He'll go.'

The policeman took a quick look round the room and didn't even seem to see them. Then he turned and went out again.

A crazy thought ran across Liam's brain. She'd made him leave. Leila had silently told the policeman to go and he'd gone.

Liam felt scared as he stepped off the bus at Nottingham. Supposing he was picked up and questioned by Inspector Dean again? Dean had almost broken him last time – and now there was so much more to hide.

As they hurried through the city he kept an eye out for patrol cars and he dodged all the CCTV cameras. Out here on the streets you had to be sharp all the time. The soft, safe life at Frazergate had sent part of him to sleep. Well, if he and Leila were going to survive, he had to wake up.

The council had started to demolish the houses in The Rat's street but his house was still standing. Liam pounded on the back door for a long time then it opened slightly and The Rat's face peered out. His eyes were bleary and his face was still creased from sleep.

'Who's she?' The Rat asked.

'A friend. She's OK.'

The Rat's eyes flicked past them to check the alleyway then he nodded and let them in. They went upstairs to the bedroom and sat on the floor while The Rat got back into his sleeping-bag. He lit a cigarette and looked at them.

'What d'you want?'

Liam told his story. He started with the day he'd last seen The Rat and went right up to the moment he and Leila had left Frazergate. He didn't mention Dr Prior, though, or why they wanted to get to France. He just hinted that they'd got fed up with school and wanted to travel for a while.

'The trouble is I haven't got a passport. Then I thought of you.'

'Passports cost – a lot!'

'We've got money,' Liam said and, seeing The Rat's eyes light up, he added, 'You'll get a cut, of course.'

'Might take a couple of days,' The Rat warned.

'That's OK. But we need somewhere to stay. Have you got room for us here? We'll pay.'

'You bet you will,' The Rat laughed. Then he grinned at Leila, 'Just one room, is it?'

'Two,' Liam said, blushing.

The Rat was out nearly all the next day seeing his contacts, but he had no luck.

'Could get hold of a Chinese passport tomorrow, but that's no good for you. Don't worry, something'll turn up.'

The hours of waiting seemed so long. There was no radio or TV in the house and nothing to read. Leila spent most of her time alone in her room and Liam felt lonely and bored. He longed to get out in the fresh air and go for a run but he was worried about being recognized. He spent ages peering out through the cracks in the boarded windows at the demolition work going on further down the road.

'What do you do all the time, stuck in your room alone?' he moaned at Leila on the third day in the house.

'I think about things.'

'Like what?'

'Human beings . . . life . . . what I have to do. It's good to have time to sort things out.'

If it had been anyone else he would have laughed and sneered, but she said it so simply and naturally that he just accepted it. She filled the time calmly and usefully while he dragged around being bored like some little kid.

That afternoon he went to his room and sat on the floor and tried to be like her. What did she think about? Life and human beings.

Well, there were two types of human beings – people like Mrs Cooper who were nice but stupid because you could take advantage of them, or hard and clever ones who knew how to look after themselves.

And as for life – you didn't ask to get born but you had to put up with it. You lived and then you died. Like Gran. All those years of filling up your time with little things and then – *Bang!* – one day you died and that was it. Gone. And the world carried on as if you'd never existed. No wonder people tried to kid themselves that there was something after death. Like that stupid vicar at Gran's funeral, going on about how they'd all meet her again in Heaven. Oh yeah! Gran was just a pile of ashes now. And stuff about 'souls' was just rubbish that people made up because they couldn't face the truth.

Surely Leila didn't have depressing thoughts like that when she did all her thinking – she wouldn't be able to stand it. Maybe she believed all that stuff about souls and Heaven.

He'd go and ask her. He crossed the corridor to Leila's room and knocked on the door. There was no answer. He knocked again and went in.

She was sitting on the floor with her back against the wall. Her eyes were closed and she was sitting still. So still that he couldn't even see her breathing. A dreadful fear gripped his heart. She looked like Gran had looked. Not just still, but empty. Not there. Gone.

He moved towards her and bent down, his heart pounding. Just as he reached out to touch her shoulder, her whole body gave a little jerk. Her faced seemed to fill with life again. She opened her eyes and looked at him.

'I thought –' he began.

'Don't ever do that!' she whispered angrily. 'Don't ever come into my room when . . . when I'm alone.'

He walked fast to the door then ran down the stairs and out of the back door. He kept running – along the alleyway and out on to the street. He didn't stop until he came to the park.

He sat on a bench and gasped air into his burning lungs. She had a nerve, talking to him like that! He hadn't done anything wrong. He ought to get out now. Leave her to sort out her own problems. She was the one who was in trouble, not him. Well, let her get on with it, without him. He'd go back to Frazergate and apologize, beg Roach to let him stay on.

But even as he was telling himself all this, he knew he wouldn't do it. It was just a sulky, childish voice in his head. He wouldn't leave her. He couldn't.

It was good to be out though, gulping down fresh air and feeling his blood still tingling from the run. He stayed and looked at the grass, so fresh and green, and the bare branches of the trees ready to burst into leaf.

'Liam, I'm sorry,' Leila said as he went in through the back door. 'I didn't mean to snap. But you must never disturb me when I'm . . . meditating. I'm sorry.'

'Yeah,' he mumbled, going straight past her, wanting to let her know that he was upset.

Again, that sulky child inside him. The sulky child stamping up the stairs and slamming the door. The sulky child slumping down on the floor and feeling sorry for himself.

And suddenly he could see himself clearly, as if he was someone else looking at this sulky child called Liam.

He knew he was playing a silly game but he couldn't stop himself. He knew he was sulking because he felt left out. Left out of something important. Something that was too grown up for sulky children like him.

And somewhere, deep down, he knew the secret that he had been left out of. The secret that was too important for sulky children to take part in.

Leila hadn't been meditating.

She hadn't been there.

One minute her body had been empty and then . . . then she had come back and filled it up again.

No, that was mad. It couldn't happen.

But it had.

Chapter Twenty-one

Liam noticed that Leila hit it off with The Rat from the very first. He was like a different person with her – laughing freely and talking to her all the time. She never asked him questions or tried to pry – all she did was listen. And the more she listened, the more he told her.

He even stopped swearing. Usually every other word was a swear word but he seemed to feel that he had to be on his best behaviour with Leila. It was as if he respected her.

And Liam knew how he felt. He respected her, too. He'd never met anyone like her before. She didn't go around being serious or anything and she didn't give herself airs but there was something about her that felt . . . different. She was straight. She was genuine. She was . . . true.

Other people played games, hid things, said one thing and meant another – himself, for instance – but she didn't. Oh, she didn't tell him everything, he was sure of that. But that was because she thought he didn't need to know. He might *want* to know but there was a big difference between need and want. Somehow, in the short time together, she had taught him that difference. And he liked knowing it. It felt like growing up a bit.

That was what was different about Leila. She was grown up. Much more than any adult he had ever met, she was grown up. And she made him feel that he would like to be too.

Not that he felt very grown up when he watched Leila with The Rat. He hated seeing how much The Rat liked her. And he hated seeing how nice she was to him and how she listened carefully to everything he said. She should be spending time with him, not with The Rat. He'd had just as hard a life as The Rat, perhaps harder.

He knew that Leila wouldn't like this sulky child part of him. She would like the part of him that tried to forget the bad things that had happened and just get on with life. He knew all that, but it didn't stop the hurting and the aching inside him.

One night he had a bad dream.

He dreamed he was inside Dr Prior's house again. He was walking towards the door and he was scared that he was going to see the body again. But what was even more scaring, he felt that he was the murderer and he didn't want to see what he had done. Then he was in the room. He couldn't really see the body but he knew it was there.

Then he forced himself to wake up because he knew that if he looked it wouldn't be Dr Prior's body, it would be The Rat's body.

He lay there in the dark and he knew he was being stupid. He was jealous. How stupid. Leila wasn't his girlfriend or anything, but he was jealous.

He even felt jealous when, on the fourth day, The Rat came racing in and went straight over to Leila.

'The Rat's got a passport!' he said with a silly excited grin on his face. '*And* he's found someone who'll take you over to France in his van. This guy does a run over there every week to buy loads of cheap booze and cigarettes to sell up here. He owes The Rat a favour so he's gonna take you. The Rat told him you wanted a cheap holiday.'

And when Leila stood up and gave The Rat a kiss on his cheek, Liam had to look away. He was the one who was supposed to be helping Leila. He was the one who'd put himself at risk at Dr Prior's house. But it was The Rat who got all the praise.

The following morning Liam went out to a photo booth to get a photo for the passport. In the afternoon

Leila carefully cut the photo of Mr Alan Royes out of the passport and replaced it with Liam's photo, covering it with a strip of sticky cellophane to match the original. Anyone who looked closely would spot what had happened but, as Leila said, they just had to hope no one looked too closely.

They had just finished the passport when The Rat burst into the room. He grabbed the passport out of Leila's hands and threw a newspaper on to the floor.

'Page Five,' he snarled.

They opened the paper.

There were two small photos of them next to a headline:

FEARS FOR DEATH SCHOOLKIDS

Two teenagers are being hunted by police after their mystery disappearance from a top private school in Sussex. Leila Khan, the daughter of a noble Indian family, and Liam Moore, an orphan, went missing during the Easter weekend.

Fears for their safety grew last night when Leila's guardian was found murdered in his luxury Chelsea house. Dr Prior's body had been mutilated and the police want to trace the missing sixteen-year-olds.

'They may have important information for us,' a CID spokesman said.

Teachers at exclusive Frazergate School were tight-lipped about the missing duo but one pupil said Moore was a loner with a bad temper. 'Leila would never go off with him willingly.'

'You should've told The Rat, you should've told him,' The Rat shouted. 'Did you do it? Did you kill him?'

'Of course we didn't kill him! It doesn't even say that,' Liam said. 'Anyway, papers get everything wrong. Look – it says we're sixteen and I'm an orphan . . .'

'You've got to go! Now!' The Rat said, grabbing hold of Liam and pulling him to his feet.

'Let go of me!' Liam yelled but The Rat continued to pull him towards the door. 'Let go!'

Liam chopped his hand down on The Rat's arm and The Rat swung round and aimed a punch at him.

'Stop it! Stop it, both of you,' Leila said, jumping to her feet and stepping between them.

'The cops are after you. It could be bad for The Rat. You've got to get out – now!'

'All right, we'll go,' Leila said. 'But we need that passport and the address of the man who's taking us across the Channel.'

'No way! The Rat's not getting involved. The Rat doesn't want trouble with the cops. The Rat –'

'You're not a rat!' Leila suddenly exploded. 'You're not a rat, you're a human being. Stop hiding behind that name. What's your real name? Come on, tell me!'

Leila was standing close to The Rat, shouting into his face. The Rat lowered his eyes, unable to meet her gaze.

'Tell me your name,' she said more quietly.

He shook his head.

She put her hands on either side of his face and raised his eyes to meet hers.

'You're not a rat. You're a person. Whatever you've done, you've done to survive,' she said.

Her voice was gentle but firm and she was looking straight into his eyes.

'You're a person. A good person. With a good heart. Tell me your name.'

The Rat opened his mouth as if he was about to say it but a soft groan came out and tears suddenly welled up in his eyes.

'Tell me . . . your . . . name,' Leila said.

'Ivan,' he whispered.

'Ivan?'

He nodded and the tears spilled down his cheeks. Leila smeared the tears away with her thumbs then took her hands away from his face.

'Ivan,' Leila went on, 'I'm asking you to help us. We need that passport and we need that man to take us in his van. And we need to stay here for the night. Will you help?'

He nodded.

'Thank you,' Leila said, then wrapped her arms round him and held on to him while he cried.

Chapter Twenty-two

As Leila and Liam sat in the back of the van on their way south, Liam thought about The Rat. Would he start using his real name now? He certainly hadn't called himself 'The Rat' or 'he' when he'd said goodbye.

'Good luck,' he'd said. 'And thanks for the money.'

'That's OK,' Leila had said. 'But listen, Ivan, use it to get a room or a flat. And start looking for a job. Promise?'

'I will, I promise,' he'd said.

Leila had given The Rat enough money for a couple of months' rent but Liam was sure he wouldn't use it to get himself settled. He wasn't like that. He didn't want a job, a proper place to live, a social security number. He would feel tied down, trapped. When they started to demolish his house he would probably find another squat and go on living as he always had.

Anyway, it was too late to worry about The Rat now. They had enough problems of their own. Their photos had been in nearly all the newspapers so the police and the immigration people were bound to be looking out for them.

'What do you reckon we ought to do? You know, when we get to the port?' he shouted to Leila above the rattling of the van.

She shook her head and smiled at him. 'It's up to you.'

'Me?' Liam gasped. 'Why?'

'Because you've got an instinct for these things.'

'What instinct?' Liam said, feeling panic rising in him.

'Some people would have been broken by what you've been through. But not you. You're tough. You know how to survive. Why do you think I asked you to help me?'

'There wasn't anyone else – that's why!'

'I didn't want anyone else. You're the one. I told you before – you're not here by chance, Liam. You've got the qualities that I need. I trust you. I can't do this without you.'

Liam was stunned into silence. She meant it. Whether she was right or wrong, Leila believed in him. She believed he had qualities. She believed he had an instinct for things. He mustn't let her down.

So, what was his instinct telling him?

Nothing.

He just wished they were in France where no one was looking for them. So far they had been lucky – the driver obviously hadn't seen their photo in the papers and he still believed they were going on a cheap holiday. He must think they were in love because he'd winked and given a dirty laugh when they said they wanted to ride in the back of the van rather than sit up front with him.

Just south of London the driver turned off the motorway and stopped at a café. He opened the back door to let them out and they crossed the lorry park towards the building. It was late at night and Liam could see there weren't many people inside. There was still a small risk that someone would recognize them but it was worth it to get something to eat and drink.

'Don't they ever stop you with all the booze and cigarettes?' Liam asked the driver as they finished eating.

'Yeah, had the whole lot confiscated once. But that's once out of nearly a hundred trips. Can't be bad.'

'So, aren't they strict with passports and things?'

'Nah, going out at this time of night the French lot usually don't give a toss. Flash a British passport at them and they just wave you through. It's the British customs that give you all the hassle when you come back in. Dead nosy lot they can be.'

As they were getting back into the van Liam suddenly had an idea.

'Can I ride up front with you? Leila wants to sleep, don't you?'

Leila looked puzzled but she nodded and got into the back of the van alone.

'Tired out already, is she?' the driver laughed, nudging Liam's arm. 'Yeah, hop in.'

The driver talked non-stop about his trips over to France and how much money he could make selling the stuff on the black market but Liam didn't really listen. He was going over his plan.

He was sure he'd made the right decision. The police would be looking for a boy and a girl together. Especially a girl with an Indian passport. This way, he and the driver could flash their British passports and get through without being stopped. With any luck, Leila wouldn't even be seen.

Liam's heart beat faster as the signs to the Channel Tunnel showed thirty miles then twenty, then ten. Finally the van filtered left off the motorway on to the slip road to the Tunnel and he could feel the dryness in his mouth and the tightness in his throat.

The driver slowed as they approached a row of ticket booths. He wound down his window.

'Day return, mate,' he said, handing the man a credit card. A minute later they had the ticket and were through the barrier.

'Is that it?' Liam asked. 'No passports?'

'Yeah, passports are up ahead.'

And then Liam saw the sign high above another set of barriers. A flashing green arrow was indicating the right-hand lane. The driver pulled over behind a couple of cars.

'Better get the girl up here now,' the driver said.

'She's asleep,' Liam said. 'They won't look in the back, will they?'

'Probably not but we don't want them thinking we're . . . Hey, hold on. They're not checking – look.'

Liam looked towards the barrier. The two officers in the booth were chatting to each other, the window was closed and they weren't even looking at the traffic.

The van drew level with the booth and still the officers weren't looking.

'Lazy gits can't be bothered,' the driver said as he accelerated forward and past the barrier. 'Be a different story coming back, I bet.'

Who cares? Liam thought, feeling a grin of relief break out on his face. His instinct had been right. They were safe. Then the grin faded as he saw another barrier ahead.

'What's that?' he asked.

'The French lot – just hold your passport up and they'll wave us through.'

But he was wrong.

The gendarme in the booth put his hand up to signal them to stop.

'Funny – never been stopped here before,' the driver said, stepping on the brake. 'Give us your passport.'

Liam's heart was pounding as he watched the driver lean out and give the two passports to the gendarme. The man flicked open the first one and glanced at the driver's face. Then he opened Liam's and looked at the photo.

A wave of heat swept up to Liam's face as the gendarme raised himself slightly to peer past the driver to get a better view. Liam looked at him and smiled but there was no answering smile in the man's eyes. They were cold and searching.

A phone rang in the booth. The gendarme picked it up.

Perhaps the phone call was from the British police. Someone had recognized him at one of the barriers.

The gendarme's eyes never left Liam and he felt they must be able to see the way his whole body was rocking with the terrified pulse of his blood.

'Allo?' the gendarme said. 'Oui . . . Non . . . D'accord . . . Attends . . .'

He handed the two passports back to the driver and jerked his head to show that they could drive on. The driver passed Liam's passport back to him then spent ages putting his own away in the glove pocket.

Liam wanted to scream at him to hurry up and drive away. The gendarme was busy chattering on the phone but he was still looking at them.

'I'll hold your passport,' Liam said, reaching over to take it.

'No, it's OK. I always keep it here,' the driver said and went on trying to jam it into the full glove pocket.

Finally he managed to wedge it in then, oh so slowly, he settled back, put the van into gear, and began to pull away from the barrier.

Ten minutes later they drove down a ramp and on to the train. Even then, Liam kept expecting something to go wrong. It wasn't until they were speeding through the tunnel under the sea that he began to believe that they were safe.

The sun was just coming up as the driver dropped them outside the station at Calais. The last they saw of him was his cheery thumbs-up out of the van window as he disappeared round a corner heading for the warehouse to load up with alcohol and cigarettes.

They bought tickets to Paris and sat in the station buffet waiting for the train to arrive. Liam ordered two coffees and four croissants and he was pleased when the lady behind the bar understood his French.

He was starving hungry and he wolfed his croissants and then ordered another one. The coffee was dark and bitter and he put a lot of sugar in it. It tasted great.

His body was still tingling from the danger and the wonderful sense of relief. Tastes and smells were so intense. Everything was different. He felt so alive.

As the train pulled into the station, Leila squeezed his arm and said, 'We've done it. I knew I could trust you. Thanks.'

Liam's heart swelled and he knew he had never been so happy in his life.

Chapter Twenty-three

Leila's contact in Paris was Ahmad Musafir. He had been born in Iraq but he'd lived in France for over forty years. He was a printer and his apartment was above his print shop in the south-eastern part of the city. It was a poor district, filled with people from North Africa and the Middle East.

Next door to Ahmad's building was an Algerian butcher who slaughtered goats and sheep in a shed in the courtyard. The stench from the dead animals drifted through the air, mixing with the smells of herbs and spices from the street market outside. The people wandering among the market stalls spoke Arabic not French and sometimes, Liam felt, it was hardly like being in Paris at all.

The arrival at Ahmad's house had been amazing. Ahmad had greeted Leila by bowing very low and kissing her hand, then he had turned to Liam and hugged him and said something in Arabic.

'He calls you "Protector" and says you are a great man,' Leila translated.

During the afternoon, as the news spread, a whole procession of people arrived to pay their respects to Leila and to greet Liam. And that evening all the visitors stayed for a feast consisting of huge bowls of rice and a whole roast lamb that the Algerian butcher slaughtered specially for the occasion.

Six days later there was another feast when Leila announced that it was their fifteenth birthday. Liam had actually lost track of the days and he hadn't even realized that it was his birthday, let alone that he shared it with Leila.

'How did you know?' he asked Leila.

'I know everything about you,' she laughed as she hung her present, a delicate gold chain, round his neck.

'You might've told me – I haven't got you anything.'

'You've given me much more than a present, Liam,' she said and stroked the side of his face with her hand. 'Born the same day. We're tied up together.'

Most of the same visitors came for the birthday feast and, again, Liam was treated like a hero. People hugged him and shook his hand and smiled at him and called him 'Protector'.

Late in the evening a couple of men started playing music on a flute and a drum. People began clapping to the rhythm and suddenly Leila came over and took hold of Liam's hands.

'Come on, let's dance.'

'No!' he said, trying to pull away. 'I can't dance!'

'Of course you can. Oh, come on, Liam. I love dancing. Please – just for me.'

She gave him such a beautiful smile that he couldn't resist and he allowed himself to be led out into the middle of the floor.

'Just move to the music,' Leila said.

She began to shuffle her feet and sway her body to the beat. He tried a couple of steps and then stopped, feeling clumsy and embarrassed.

'Come on, it's easy,' Leila said, putting her hands round the back of his neck and rocking him gently from side to side.

By now other people were getting up and dancing so, bit by bit, Liam relaxed. He listened to the notes of the flute weaving in and out of the heartbeat of the drum and when Leila let go of him he went on dancing.

He couldn't take his eyes off her. She danced so well. Her whole body was filled with the rhythm of the music.

She was so supple and graceful. Every bend of her arm, every sway of her back, every shuffling step was saying, 'I'm young! I'm alive! And life is wonderful!'

And suddenly Liam couldn't help himself. He laughed out loud. Laughed in sheer pleasure. Pleasure in the music, and in dancing, and in Leila, and in being alive.

She heard him laugh and she laughed too. And they went on laughing and dancing while the music throbbed and vibrated through them.

The next day he was looking out of the window early in the morning when he saw Leila leave the house and get into a chauffeur-driven Mercedes. The car brought her back late in the afternoon. Liam asked where she'd been.

'Oh, there was a meeting,' she said vaguely.

From then on, Liam hardly got a chance to talk to her because the car called for her nearly every day. And when she wasn't out she had an endless stream of visitors, mostly mothers and fathers with young children and babies. She sat in Ahmad's living-room and chatted with the parents in Arabic then, just before they left, she would take the child on her lap and say something that sounded like a prayer.

'Why do they all bring their kids to you?' Liam asked.

Leila paused before she said, 'They want me to bless them.'

'Bless them? What are you, some kind of priest or princess or something?'

'Of course not,' she smiled. 'It's just that there have been a lot of great and wise teachers in my family. People bring their children to me because they want them to come into contact with all that.'

'Oh, so you're great and wise then, are you?' Liam asked sarcastically.

'What do you think?' Leila laughed, as if it was a stupid idea.

*

The next day the car picked her up early in the morning as usual. As he watched it drive away, Liam decided to go out. He couldn't stand the thought of another day alone in the house so he made up his mind to start exploring Paris on his own.

Day after day he went into the centre of the city and walked round looking at the crowds and the shops. He was pleased with his progress in French and it was exciting to be in a foreign country. Most of the time he could lose himself in the bustle and forget everything but sometimes he couldn't help feeling angry at Leila.

Why did she spend all her time with other people when she could be with him? He was the one who'd got her out of England. She owed him. And he had the right to know what was going on. And why the hell were they hanging around in Paris? Why weren't they moving on to Morocco like she said?

At times like these he vowed that he would ask her and make her answer. He never did, though, because something kept reminding him about the difference between wanting to know and needing to know. It hurt not to ask, but it felt grown up. And he wanted Leila to think he was grown up, even if it wasn't true.

And then something happened that meant he had to ask.

He was passing a kiosk in the street when he saw their photos on the front page of a French newspaper.

Chapter Twenty-four

'We should've kept going instead of hanging around here. We could've been in Morocco by now,' Liam said to Leila when she finished reading the newspaper report. 'It's your fault!'

'I had work to do here,' she replied.

'What work?'

'I've been talking to groups of people, explaining things to them.'

'What things?'

'I can't tell you.'

'Why not?' he snapped. 'Why can't you tell me? You talk to groups of people, why the hell don't you talk to me? Who are they anyway? Friends or what?'

'Friends? I suppose you could call them that.'

'Yeah, well, someone told the papers we're here in Paris. How do you know it wasn't one of your so-called friends?'

'I don't,' she said coolly.

'I thought you knew everything,' he said bitterly.

She smiled and put her hand on his shoulder.

'I'm like you, Liam. I know what I need to know. Perhaps you're right – perhaps one of the people here did tell the papers. If they did, I don't know why. Perhaps it's important that we get publicity so that people hear about our journey together.'

'What? You're mad! You're bloody mad!' Liam yelled, shrugging her hand off his shoulder.

He was so angry and so confused that he had to stand up and walk around. He felt like hitting her and had to move to stop himself doing it.

'You're mad!' he yelled again, trying to let his anger out. 'The cops think we killed Doctor Prior. And you want publicity!'

'I didn't say I wanted publicity. I said perhaps it was part of the plan.'

'What plan? What plan? Tell me!' he screamed, grabbing hold of her and shaking her.

There was a jagged explosion in his arms as if a bolt of electricity had surged out of her. The charge of power shot through him, jerking his hands away from her.

'I can't tell you,' she said quietly as if nothing had happened.

A mixture of shame and rage sent him racing across the room and down the stairs. He hated himself for grabbing her like that, grabbing her and shaking her the way his mother used to shake him, wanting to hit her the way his mother used to hit him. He hated it.

He crashed open the door and ran out on to the street. He blundered through the evening crowds until he came to the Metro station. When he turned round from buying his ticket, Leila was standing there.

'Let's talk,' she said and he found himself numbly following her back up the stairs to the street level.

She led him to the local park and for a long while they walked silently along the gravel paths beneath the chestnut trees. Finally she sat down on a bench and he sat beside her. A small chestnut blossom had fallen on her hair.

'All right, what do you want to know?' she asked.

There were so many questions whirling around in his head. So many questions. But there was one that covered them all.

'Tell me what the plan is,' he said.

'You won't believe me.'

'Why?'

'Because it is to do with the Secret That Conceals Itself.'

'What the hell does that mean?'

'It means that it's a secret that stays secret because no one believes it.'

'Tell me,' he said.

Leila got up from the bench and walked away. She stood looking down the alley of chestnut trees for a moment then she came back. She sat down.

'OK, I'll tell you.' She took a deep breath and looked at him. 'There are certain people on this planet who are not like ordinary human beings. They are in touch with another dimension – a world that is hidden from us. They know what humanity's destiny is and they try to guide human beings in the right direction.'

'Oh yeah! And they've got pointy little heads and they took you for a ride in one of their flying saucers!'

'I told you that you wouldn't believe it,' Leila said.

Liam picked up a handful of gravel and began throwing the small stones at a stick on the far side of the path. He'd made the silly joke because he didn't want her to go on. He didn't want to hear this stuff. His hand was trembling so badly that the stones weren't going anywhere near the stick.

He couldn't believe her, he just couldn't.

But what about all the strange things that happened around her? He opened his hand and let the rest of the gravel trickle through his fingers.

'All right,' he said. 'So supposing there are these special people. Are you one of them?'

'No. But I'm connected to them. They can't interfere directly in human affairs so they have to work through ordinary people who understand what they're trying to do. They give these people a special education that prepares them to take part in The Work. People in my family have been involved in this for hundreds of years.'

'Just your family?'

'No. Many, many people have spread the ideas throughout history. Some have been famous – leaders, artists, great thinkers, inventors – but most have been unknown people who worked so quietly that even their neighbours didn't know what they were doing.'

'Why do they keep it quiet? They ought to teach everybody if it's so damned important,' Liam cut in.

'One day they will. But knowledge of these things brings enormous power.'

'What kind of power?'

'Well, power over other people's minds for example. Just imagine you could make someone do anything you wanted. Look in your heart, Liam – can you be sure you wouldn't misuse that power?'

He shook his head.

'No,' Leila said. 'And at least you realize it. Most people wouldn't even admit it about themselves. Luckily there's a kind of safety lock on the knowledge – it can only be learned by people who can control their desires and their emotions. Human beings think they are so advanced but they're still living in darkness. The Work helps to change people so that they're ready to learn.'

'Are you one of these helpers who've had this special education?' Liam asked.

Leila nodded.

A sudden extraordinary thought struck Liam.

'You didn't learn all this at Frazergate, did you?' he asked in astonishment.

There was a wild burst of laughter from Leila and after a couple of seconds Liam joined in. And the more he thought about Mr Roach and the other teachers at Frazergate, the more ridiculous his question seemed and the more he laughed.

The laughter made him feel good. It cleared the air between them. She might be some kind of special person but they could still laugh together. She was still the Leila that he'd known before.

He'd been scared because it all sounded so weird, but the fact that she could laugh about it made it easier to accept. After all, it was only like a religion and people believed all sorts of strange things in religions. It didn't mean that *he* had to believe it.

But the scary thing was that there was so much that backed up what she was saying. The way she could read his mind, for example. And that strange day when she seemed to have left her body. And the fact that people were trying to kill her. Of course, people from different religions often killed each other – perhaps it was that.

'Why do these people want to kill you?'

'Because in the same way that there are people who want to help bring human beings out of the darkness, so there are forces that want to keep them there. They want to destroy The Work.'

'Yeah, but why you? What have you done to them?'

'Nothing. But ever since I was born, my destiny has been linked with The Keeper of the Age.'

'Who the hell's that?'

'I don't know who it is. I just know that there is always a Keeper of the Age alive on the planet. If there wasn't, none of this work could go on. Without The Keeper of the Age the forces of destruction and chaos would win and this planet would cease to exist.'

'Oh come on! You can't believe that!'

'I don't believe it, I know it,' she said. 'I'm part of a plan to protect The Keeper of the Age. And perhaps that's why we need to have publicity about our journey – to act as a sort of decoy.'

'And what about me? Why am I mixed up in it?'

'Because your destiny is tied up with mine. You've got qualities that I need. You can do things that I can't. Without you, I will fail.'

She'd gone really over the top with this stuff about The Keeper of the Age – that was even weirder than most religions – but he didn't care. He wanted his destiny to be tied up with hers. It meant that she needed him. No one had ever needed him before and he loved the feeling it gave him.

She might have all these weird ideas but she *was* a special person. It was obvious. All the people round her treated her like one. Even The Rat had sensed it. But, more important than that, Liam felt it. Deep in his heart he knew that she was special.

If she wanted to go to Morocco, they would go there. And if there had to be publicity that made their journey harder, then he would accept it.

And he would never be jealous of other people even if she spent more time with them than she did with him. Because now he was sure. She needed him. Their destinies were tied up together.

It was better than family; better than boyfriend and girlfriend.

He was linked to her, heart and soul.

Chapter Twenty-five

Now that the police knew they were in Paris Liam wanted to leave at once but Leila said they had to stay for a few weeks longer. He knew it was dangerous but he'd vowed that he wouldn't argue with her so he didn't say anything.

Every day the big Mercedes arrived to take Leila to her meetings but Liam stayed indoors in case he was recognized. Finally, though, he became so bored that he put on some dark glasses and a baseball cap and went out on to the streets again. He felt nervous at first but no one paid any attention to him so he went back to exploring the city.

He had just begun to think that perhaps the whole thing had been forgotten by the press when two new photographs of them appeared on the front cover of a magazine. Leila was smiling her beautiful smile but his photo was horrible. It had been taken by the Social Services when he went to Beeches Hall and it made him look angry and slightly mad. The title above the photos was '*Jeunes Assassins*'.

The article was about violence among young people and it gave examples of terrible events from all over the world. The last couple of paragraphs were all about Dr Prior. They went into gruesome detail about the murder and strongly hinted that the police thought that Liam and Leila were the killers.

Liam stopped going out of the house again.

The hours passed slowly when Leila was out. He read the newspapers every day to try to improve his French and to check that there were no further articles about them. Then he often went downstairs to the printing shop. Ahmad was friendly but he was usually busy and the clatter of the old-fashioned printing presses made it difficult to chat very much.

Since early May, Paris had sweltered in a heatwave. When it got really hot in the afternoons Liam liked to go up to the flat roof of the building. Ahmad had made a small terrace up there with a couple of potted palm trees as rather pathetic reminders of his desert birthplace. The sun beat down fiercely but there was usually a cooling breeze and there were wonderful views over the shimmering city towards the white shape of the church of Sacré-Coeur far away to the north.

At the back of the building he could look down at the courtyard of Karim, the Algerian butcher. He couldn't actually see into the small shed where the animals were killed but he could see the sheep and goats as they were pulled inside. He could hear their panic-stricken squeals as they were hung upside down and their throats were cut. Blood often ran out through the door and Karim always emerged with his knives and arms splattered with it.

Liam knew that the way the animals were killed was part of a religious belief and it was probably less cruel than what happened in big abattoirs but it still made him shiver each time he saw it. He hated the stench of blood and innards that drifted up on the hot afternoon air. And he couldn't help it, he disliked Karim with his dark, sunken eyes and his huge moustache. He was a chilling reminder that death was always so close.

It was a relief to hurry across to the other side of the roof and look down at the bustle of the street market. The noise from the milling crowds, the colour, the energy, and the sweet spicy smells – that was life.

One day Liam was surprised to see that the street was almost empty. He wondered if it was a religious holiday and he went down to ask Ahmad.

'They're frightened,' Ahmad shouted above the noise of the print shop. 'Big trouble in another market yesterday. Racists who want Arabs out of France, they attacked the traders, knocked over the stalls and burned the goods. Bad times.'

That night Liam found it difficult to get to sleep. His room was stuffy so he got up to open the window. As he stood there, cooling off and gazing at the huge full moon that hung above the rooftops, he heard a noise from the courtyard below. He looked down and saw a shadowy figure coming out of the slaughter shed.

The figure moved slowly to the wall. There was a streak of reflected moonlight and Liam saw a long butcher's knife held up and placed on top of the wall. A moment later Karim's face came out of the shadows as he raised himself up next to the knife. He straddled the wall, grabbed the knife, and lowered himself down into Ahmad's courtyard.

Chapter Twenty-six

Liam pulled on his jeans and T-shirt, jammed his bare feet into his shoes, and crept down the stairs to the print shop. He made his way past the printing presses and out into the corridor that led to the back door. He turned the latch silently and stood for a moment, breathing deeply, before he jerked the door open.

He'd expected to see the butcher standing there with his knife but the courtyard was empty. He held his breath and listened. There were faint footsteps from the alleyway and he saw that the courtyard door was open. He tiptoed across and peered out. Karim was walking fast towards the end of the alley.

Liam waited until he was sure the butcher had reached the street then he ran after him. As he came out on to the pavement, Liam saw Karim standing on the other side of the road looking up at Leila's window.

'What are you doing?' Liam called and then, realizing he'd spoken in English, he repeated the question in French.

The butcher put his finger to his lips and beckoned with his other hand. The blade of the knife flashed in the moonlight as he waved his hand. Liam pointed to the knife and shook his head.

The butcher looked down at the knife and then looked up again. A huge grin showed white under his black moustache. He knelt and sent the knife skidding across the surface of the road. Liam put his foot on it as it spun towards him, then he bent down and picked it up. It was heavy and its blade was razor sharp. He crossed the road, holding the knife out in front of him, and stopped well short of the butcher in case he had another one hidden away.

'I had a phone call,' Karim said softly. 'A friend tells me there will be trouble. The knife is protection. For her.'

Karim lifted his eyes briefly towards Leila's window and Liam felt he was telling the truth. There was no madness or cruelty in the eyes, only concern.

'What kind of trouble?' Liam asked, stepping closer and lowering the knife.

'Racists,' the butcher said, then he stopped and moved his head to listen to something. Liam heard it too – the sound of speeding cars.

'Quick,' Karim said, grabbing hold of Liam's arm and pulling him into a shop doorway.

The roar of the engines grew closer then, with a squeal of tyres, two cars turned into the street. Liam heard them stop and he peered round the edge of the doorway. Four men jumped out of the cars. Two of them ran across the road, took out some cans, and began spraying slogans on a wall. The other two pulled long crowbars out of one of the cars and stood waiting.

As soon as the spraying was finished the other men stepped forward and swung the crowbars. A couple of shop windows shattered and while glass was still crashing to the ground the men raced to the cars and jumped in. The cars shot forward and Liam pressed himself back into the shadows of the doorway, expecting them to speed past. There was another screech of brakes, though, and the cars skidded to a halt almost opposite him.

The four men leapt from the cars and the two with the crowbars walked up to the windows of Ahmad's print shop and smashed them. The other two men held up bottles with rags stuffed into the neck. A match flared and the rags caught light. The men raised the flaming bottles and tossed them through the broken window. There was a faint clink and then a sheet of fire exploded inside.

Karim grabbed the knife from Liam's hand and surged past him out of the doorway. The men were already scrambling back into the cars and the engines were racing but the butcher charged across the road towards them with the knife raised above his head.

The first car shot away before he could reach it but he hurled himself in front of the second car as it started to move. The driver revved the engine and drove straight at him. Karim tried to leap out of the way but the wing of the car smashed into his side, sending him cartwheeling on to the pavement.

As the cars disappeared down the road, Liam ran across to the butcher. He was struggling to sit up and Liam knelt down and put his arm round his shoulders to help him. Karim groaned and clenched his teeth and Liam looked down and saw why. His left leg was broken. A jagged end of shin-bone had ripped through the flesh and was sticking out just below his knee. Blood was soaking his jeans.

'Lie still,' Liam said, lowering him back to the ground.

'Leave me,' the butcher gasped and nodded towards the fire. 'Get Leila.'

Liam ran towards Ahmad's shop and looked through the window. The two petrol bombs had set the floor alight round the printing presses. Sheets of paper were swirling up into the air as the draught of the fire caught them and set them alight. Flames were scorching the large drums of ink and the canisters of alcohol used for cleaning the presses. At any moment the whole place would go up like an inferno.

There were still no flames at the near end of the room, though, and he could just see the staircase through the smoke. If he went now he might be able to get upstairs before it was too late. He jumped through the broken window and made for the stairs.

The heat was terrible. He had only taken a couple of paces when he felt his eyebrows start to singe, then the ends of his long hair crackled and caught fire. He kept moving, though, and burst through the flames to the staircase. He ran up the stairs beating his burning hair with his hands.

As he reached the first-floor corridor he stopped and felt the charred ends of his hair. His right ear had been burned but his hair was no longer alight.

The smoke was thicker up here and he could hardly see his way along the corridor to the next staircase. His eyes stung and he began to cough. Suddenly a figure blundered out of the smoke towards him. It was Ahmad and he was cradling a small fire extinguisher against his chest.

'It's no good. The fire's too big,' Liam shouted but Ahmad brushed past him and disappeared into the smoke billowing up from the shop.

Liam felt his way along the corridor and up the next staircase. The smoke thinned when he reached the top and he could see that Leila's door was still closed. For a moment he remembered the last time he'd burst in on her and he almost raised his hand to knock but then he grabbed the handle and pushed the door open.

Leila was fully dressed and she was sitting on her bed with her large bag on her lap as if she'd known he would come and was calmly waiting for him. A strange mix of anger and pride swept through him.

'Come on! Get out!' he yelled, letting the anger take over.

She stood up and walked steadily towards him – no panic, no fear.

As they reached the doorway there was a loud crump and the building shook. A ball of flame whirled along the corridor below. The ink and alcohol had exploded in the shop. If Ahmad was down there he must surely be dead.

'This way!' Liam shouted, grabbing the bag from Leila.

They ran along the short passageway and up the narrow stairs that led to the roof. The door had a lock and two bolts. Thick black smoke was starting to billow round them and Liam's lungs were choking as he turned the key and reached up to slide open the top bolt.

Now for the bottom bolt.

He felt Leila slump against him as he searched for the bolt in the blinding, stinging smoke. Then his fingers found it and he slid it back.

The door swung open and he threw the bag on to the flat roof and stumbled after it, pulling Leila with him. They gasped fresh air into their lungs and began coughing. There was a whooshing sound behind them and flames shot out from the doorway.

Still coughing, they staggered to the edge of the roof and clambered over the parapet on to Karim's building. His rooftop door was locked but one of the panels was loose so Liam kicked it in and bent down and reached up to open the latch.

They ran down the stairs, through the shop, and out on to the pavement.

The butcher was still lying on the ground and his wife and son were bending down next to him, holding his hands. Liam and Leila ran over and he opened his eyes.

'Allah be praised!' Karim sighed as he saw Leila, then he rolled his head round to look at Liam. 'The Protector!'

There was a shuffling sound behind them and Ahmad came limping towards them. His clothes were torn and blackened and his face and head were covered in blisters and charred flesh where his hair and beard had been burned off. But he was alive.

He slumped to his knees in front of Leila.

'Explosion,' he murmured thickly, barely able to move his blistered lips. 'I was in the corridor. It blew me through the back window.'

'Oh, Ahmad, it's because of me,' Leila said, kneeling down next to him and putting her arm round his shoulders.

'No matter,' Ahmad managed to say. 'You're safe. The Work goes on.'

Liam saw Leila's lips tremble and he thought she would break into tears but she looked tenderly at Ahmad for a moment then she nodded.

'Yes,' she said. 'The Work goes on.'

The sound of a siren cut through the roar of the fire.

'Go,' Ahmad croaked and then winced as his swollen lip split open.

'We can't leave you now,' Liam said.

'Yes, the police will come. You must go,' Ahmad whispered.

The police. Liam had forgotten. Suddenly the sound of the siren seemed louder and more urgent.

Leila lifted Ahmad's hand and placed it against her forehead.

'Thank you,' she said.

She let go of Ahmad and walked over to Karim.

'Thank you,' she said again.

'We have been blessed by your presence,' Karim's wife said.

Leila smiled gently and put her hand on Karim's son's head then she turned and strode back to Liam.

'Let's go,' she said.

They ran to the corner just as the fire engines and police cars turned into the other end of the road.

Five blocks away they stopped and looked up at the night sky. Sparks from the fire at Ahmad's house were floating up into the darkness over the rooftops. Smoke and ash hung in the air smudging the huge silver moon.

Chapter Twenty-seven

Leila stopped at a phone booth and rang a number. Half an hour later the big Mercedes drew up and the chauffeur drove them to a beautiful house off the Champs-Elysées.

The chauffeur showed them to their rooms. Liam's bedroom was the biggest he'd ever seen. There was a four-poster bed and dark old-fashioned furniture and it seemed more like a museum than a bedroom. He opened an oak-panelled door and found that he had his own private bathroom. He took a cool shower, dried himself on an enormous white towel, got into bed, and curled up on the plump feather mattress.

Only a couple of hours ago he'd been trying to get to sleep in a stuffy little bedroom in one of the poorest parts of town and now here he was in luxury. And what about Ahmad and Karim? Were they both lying in some hospital bed by now?

He thought about Ahmad's burnt face and he shivered in horror as he remembered Karim's bone sticking out through the skin. And where were the men who'd started the fire? Were they sitting together, laughing about it and feeling proud of what they'd done?

Of all the houses in Paris they'd had to go and choose Ahmad's place. It was really bad luck. As if he and Leila didn't have enough trouble already. It was like being cursed, he thought as he turned over and closed his eyes.

He felt the softness of the bed pulling his exhausted body down into sleep.

Leila woke him next morning and led him down the wide staircase to the kitchen. A housekeeper put a pot of coffee and a basket of bread and croissants on the table and then left them alone to eat.

'Is this where you've been coming for your meetings?' Liam asked.

Leila nodded.

'God, who lives here? Must be a millionaire.'

'He's a diplomat. The house doesn't belong to him. It goes with the job.'

'A diplomat! How do you know him?'

'He's an old friend of my family's.'

'Oh,' Liam said and he felt a strange hollow of disappointment open up inside him. If the diplomat was in contact with her family, it must mean that the journey was over. He would tell her parents where she was and they would come and take her home to safety.

Liam poured himself another bowl of coffee and sat stirring it, lost in his thoughts. It was great for Leila, of course, but what would it mean for him?

'What?' he asked when he looked up and saw Leila smiling at him.

'Nothing's changed, Liam,' she said with a little laugh in her voice.

'How do you – ?' he began.

'I'm not going home,' she cut in. 'Nothing's changed. I still have to go to Morocco and I still need you to help me get there. I wanted to stay here a bit longer but it's too dangerous now.'

'Why?'

'You saw what happened last night. Those men didn't fire-bomb Ahmad's house by chance.'

'You mean they were after you?'

'No. They don't even know who I am. If you asked them why they chose that particular house they wouldn't know.'

'I don't get it. What's it got to do with you, then?'

'They were being used. They didn't care which houses or shops they smashed or burned as long as they belonged to Arabs. But they were *made* to choose Ahmad's house.'

'Made to? Who by?'

'By the forces that want to destroy me. They used the hatred and anger of the men and directed it towards me.'

'Oh, come off it! You're just being paranoid!'

'It's not paranoid. I'm telling you the truth,' Leila said simply, getting up and taking her plate and bowl across to the sink. 'People often do things without knowing the real reason why. Suppose you're feeling generous and you decide to give some money to someone who's homeless. Why do you decide to give to this one rather than another one?'

'Chance. The first one I see – I don't know.'

'Yes, most of the time it's like that,' Leila said. 'But sometimes it isn't. Sometimes you are "nudged" to give it to the second homeless person you see rather than the first one. Your generosity has been directed.'

'Who by?'

'By forces. Forces that can see that your generosity is really needed by that second person. Last night, the anger and hatred of those racists was used by forces and directed against me.'

'That's just crap!'

'Look,' Leila said, holding up a plate. 'If I let go of this, it would drop to the floor. Why?'

'Because of gravity.'

'Exactly – because of a force called gravity. You can't see or hear or touch gravity so how do you know it's there?'

'I learned about it at school.'

'OK, but three hundred years ago they didn't teach gravity in schools because most people didn't know it existed. Well, I'm telling you about another force, one that they don't teach you about in schools because most people don't know it exists yet. There are all kinds of forces at work in the universe that human beings don't know about yet.'

Liam didn't know what to say and he felt a swirl of anger and doubt and confusion sweep through him. How could he believe all this stuff? And yet it was strange that the men had chosen Ahmad's house. And what had he ended up feeling, just before he went to sleep last night? That he and Leila were cursed. Well, the idea of being cursed was even weirder than what she was saying.

Leila finished washing up her breakfast things and came over to him at the table. She put her hands on his shoulders and all his anger and doubt seemed to slip away. He wished she would put her arms round him and hug him tight.

'Can you be ready in an hour?' she asked and squeezed his shoulders gently. 'I've got one last meeting this morning and then we're leaving.'

'Where are we going?' he asked, wanting to turn his head and kiss her hand.

'Spain,' she said, letting go of him.

'How?'

'By car. It's all arranged.'

Chapter Twenty-eight

Liam went up to his bedroom and lay down on the bed, waiting. He heard a number of people arrive and go into one of the rooms below. Part of him longed to find out what went on at Leila's meetings and he was tempted to go down and listen at the door. Perhaps she was telling them secrets, answers to the questions that churned around in his head. But he knew it would be wrong to eavesdrop. He closed the door and tried to concentrate on reading a magazine.

An hour later he heard the people leaving and he couldn't resist going on to the landing and looking down at the big hall below. About a dozen men and women were standing there chatting. They looked ordinary and not at all weird. The only unusual thing was that, as each of them left, they bowed to Leila and kissed her hand.

When they had all gone, Leila knocked on a door which opened to reveal a tall, grey-haired man wearing an elegant suit. He looked Middle Eastern with his olive skin and dark eyes and Liam realized he must be the diplomat who lived there.

Leila stood talking to him for a couple of minutes then he knelt down in front of her. She placed her hand on the top of his head for a few moments then he stood up again. He bowed deeply to her then she turned and started up the stairs.

Liam tiptoed back to his room and a moment later Leila knocked on the door and said it was time to go. They went down to the garage in the basement of the house where the chauffeur was waiting for them in the

Mercedes. They put their belongings in the boot and then got into the back of the car.

'We're going to have to hide until we're clear of Paris – just in case,' Leila said, lying on the floor and indicating that Liam should do the same. The chauffeur threw a blanket over them then started the car and drove out on to the city streets.

It was hot and stuffy under the blanket and it was over an hour before the car stopped in a parking area on the autoroute. The chauffeur pulled the blanket off them and they were able to sit up on the comfortable leather seats.

The chauffeur's name was André and as they headed south, he told them about his years of driving. He'd been a long-distance lorry driver for twenty-seven years before becoming a chauffeur and he reckoned that, adding it all up, he'd covered nearly five million kilometres on the roads of France.

'I know all the short cuts and the best cafés in every town,' he laughed.

They drove solidly until late afternoon and then stopped at a service station just south of Lyon. Liam and Leila stayed in the car while André went into the shop to buy drinks and sandwiches for them.

They set off again and Leila fell asleep. The warm sunlight lit up her lovely face and a stray lock of her hair fluttered back and forth across her forehead as the wind streamed in from the open window. Her head slid to one side as the car jolted so Liam rolled up the blanket into a pillow and put it on the seat next to him.

'Lie down, you'll be more comfortable,' he said, pulling her gently.

'Thanks,' she murmured as she opened her eyes briefly and curled up across the seat.

The top of her head pressed against his leg and he could feel the warmth of it through his jeans. He sat looking down at her, trying to imprint a picture of her face in his brain so that he would never forget it – the long eyelashes, the downward curve of her nose, the delicate brown of her smooth skin and the lips that tilted in a slight smile even in her sleep.

André drove fast and Liam noted the names of the towns on the autoroute signs – Valence, Montélimar, Orange, Nîmes. The further south they got the drier the countryside became and the air felt much warmer even though the sun was beginning to set.

They stopped again near Montpellier for petrol and another snack. André needed a rest so he lay down across the front seats and promptly fell asleep. There wasn't much danger of being recognized in the growing darkness so Liam and Leila strolled round the large parking area for half an hour. Then they sat near the roadside listening to the chirping of the crickets and watching the headlights of the cars racing past.

'Where are we going in Spain?' Liam asked.

'Sepudillo. It's a small place north of Madrid. There are some people there we can stay with for a while.'

'Friends?'

'I've never met them. But they're friends, yes.'

When they got back to the car André had woken up and was ready to go. Liam asked to borrow a couple of maps and he studied them as they drove on towards Spain. He found Sepudillo on the map then he traced the route they would probably take to get there.

He kept looking back to the line on the map that marked the frontier between France and Spain. If they kept on this autoroute they would cross it at a small place called Le Perthus. He stared at the map, trying to picture the border post – probably with two sets of controls, one French and one Spanish.

It was the quickest and most obvious route to take but the more he looked at the map the more uneasy he became. There was a tightening in his chest and he suddenly had a terrible feeling that they were going to be caught.

It was a ridiculous fear, of course, and he tried to put it out of his mind by listening to Leila and André. They had just passed the town of Béziers and the two of them were talking about a massacre that had taken place there hundreds of years ago. Leila seemed to know all about it.

'They were massacred because they understood about some of the hidden forces at work in the universe,' she said and glanced at Liam. 'The Church thought they were a threat to its power, so they wiped them out – men, women and children.'

Liam had seen Leila's glance and knew what it meant but he didn't bother to say anything. No matter how he tried, he couldn't stop thinking about the frontier.

He looked at the map again. About thirty kilometres east of the autoroute there was another border crossing on the small coastal road near Cerbère. The tight knot in his chest relaxed – they could go that way. He looked back at the main crossing and the knot was back again. It was stupid – how could he get a feeling like this just by looking at a map? But no matter how stupid it was, the feeling just wouldn't go away.

For nearly an hour he tried to ignore the lump of tension inside him but as they got closer to the last exit before the frontier he couldn't stand it any longer.

'I think we ought to get off this road and go this way,' he said to Leila, showing her the map.

'Why?' she asked, looking at him closely.

'I've just got a feeling . . .'

Leila started to smile and he thought she was going to laugh at him but then he saw that it wasn't a mocking smile at all – she was smiling with pleasure, as if he had done something good.

'Trust your intuition, Liam,' she said then leaned forward and asked André to get off at the next exit.

Two minutes later they left the autoroute and headed towards the sea.

The coastal road twisted and turned up over the cliffs and they kept getting glimpses of the Mediterranean shimmering in the moonlight. They passed through the small town of Cerbère and, following the signs to Spain, started up the hill towards the frontier.

As they left Cerbère behind Liam suddenly felt the knot begin to twist inside him again.

They were going to be caught.

What an idiot! He'd made them turn off the autoroute because of some silly panic inside him and now here it was again. He couldn't make them stop this time. And yet the feeling was growing in him.

They were going to be caught.

His heart had started to race and something inside him was almost screaming at him not to go on.

The lights of the frontier were visible up ahead. In a minute they would be there. And they would be caught. He was sure of it.

But he couldn't say anything. Not this time.

Fight this wild panic. Of course they wouldn't be caught.

Trust your intuition, Leila had said.

He could see the frontier clearly now, the French and Spanish flags, flying side by side in the lights.

'Stop the car!' he shouted and André stamped on the brake.

Chapter Twenty-nine

Once they'd taken the decision to turn round and go back to Cerbère, all of Liam's fears disappeared. He felt clear-headed and determined. He was sure they had done the right thing; now it was up to him to decide what to do next.

André and Leila stayed in the car while he walked down to the beach. There were three upturned boats on the shingle and he sat on one of them for a couple of minutes and then went down to the water's edge. He picked up some pebbles, and began throwing them into the sea as he went through the situation in his mind.

There was no point in trying any other crossing points along the frontier – if it was dangerous here, it was dangerous everywhere. So they would have to go where there were no border checks, no passport controls – after all it wasn't as if there was some kind of barrier all along the frontier. They could head out over the hills and cross into Spain on foot. Then they could meet up with André on the other side.

He picked up a flat round stone and, taking careful aim, sent it spinning towards the sea. It hit perfectly and as it bounced and skimmed . . . three . . . four . . . five . . . six times across the moonlit water another idea came to him.

He ran back up the beach and lifted each of the boats and looked under them.

'Damn!'

He looked around.

There was a long storebox over by the sea wall. He ran across to it but there was a padlock on the lid.

'André, I need your help,' he said when he got back to the car. 'What tools have you got in the boot?'

Liam had hoped there might be a crowbar or a hacksaw but he had to settle for a wheel brace and a hammer.

'What are you doing?' Leila called from the car as he headed back to the beach with André.

'Just stay there,' Liam called back.

Best not to let her know until it was too late to stop him.

He told André his plan though, and he was pleased when the chauffeur nodded and said, 'Good idea. Let's get on with it.'

The thud of the hammer and the screech of the wood as Liam began prising the lock away sounded terribly loud in the darkness. He and André looked anxiously towards the café a couple of hundred metres away along the seafront. The late-night drinkers at the bar were still chatting happily to each other. One last clout with the hammer and the lid was undone. Liam lifted it and pulled out two of the oars.

He carried them down and put them in one of the boats then he and André pulled it across the shingle to the water's edge.

On the way back to the car, André stopped next to the storebox and pulled out some money from his wallet.

'That'll make up for the inconvenience,' he said, dropping the notes into the box. 'And the fishermen on the Spanish side are sure to let them know that the boat's been found.'

When they got back to the car, Liam pulled their travel bag out of the boot.

'This way there's nothing to connect us with you,' he said to André.

André nodded. 'I'll meet you on the other side at six tomorrow morning.'

'Are you going to tell me what's happening?' Leila said as she got out of the car.

'Yes, we're going to Spain. Follow me.'

He set off fast across the road and down the steps on to the beach. By the time Leila had caught up with him he had already stowed the bag and was pushing the boat into the sea.

'Liam, what are you doing?' she asked angrily.

At that moment headlights from a car began to run across the beach like a searchlight.

'Just get in quick!' he yelled as the lights swept towards them.

The urgency in his voice had its effect and Leila jumped into the boat without another word. He pushed hard on the stern and the boat grated and crunched over the pebbles and into the water. He waded into the sea, still pushing, and then swung his leg up and rolled into the boat.

He staggered to the centre of the rocking boat, fell on to a seat, then grabbed the oars and began rowing. When he looked back at the shore, the beach was still deserted. No one was running after them. The car had stopped at the café and the driver was slowly getting out for a late-night drink with friends.

Liam pulled easily and strongly on the oars for nearly forty-five minutes and then stopped for a breather. They had rounded the headland and could no longer see the lights of Cerbère. To the left, the cliffs of Cap Cerbère loomed darkly over them. Somewhere, up there, was the frontier post. It wasn't likely that anyone kept a permanent watch over the sea, but Liam was grateful that the moon was hidden behind the tall cliffs and that the boat was in shadow.

He was also grateful for all the training he'd done during the winter. All that running and all those hours in the gym were paying off now in the power he felt in his shoulders as he began pulling on the oars again. If only

115

he'd thought of toughening up his hands – the blisters were starting to swell already.

Half an hour later they could see the lights of Port-Bou. They were in Spanish waters.

Liam kept the boat well out at sea until they had passed the harbour of Port-Bou and were at the far end of the bay. He then pulled heavily on the right-hand oar and began to row towards the shore.

The boat glided on to the beach and they jumped overboard and pulled it well clear of the water. There was no one about as they ran up the beach and climbed the steps to the promenade.

They walked quickly through the sleeping town in the direction of the frontier. The road climbed up the cliffs and as soon as they were clear of the houses they turned on to a strip of rough ground. Gorse bushes scratched them as they made their way through the scrub towards the cliff top but they soon came to a small clearing. They rolled up a couple of sweaters as pillows and lay down to try to get some sleep.

Liam ached badly when Leila woke him in the morning but the sun was rising and its warmth soothed him when he stood up and stretched. He looked at his watch – five-thirty. They would have to hurry.

It was a steep climb up to the frontier and they were both sweating by the time they got there. They stopped about a hundred metres from it and almost immediately saw the black Mercedes approaching from the French side. There was one car in front of it and the first driver slowed and stopped at the control booth. He held out his identity card and was waved on.

The Mercedes rolled forward and they saw André hold out his identity card. At that moment, a police car, which had been parked next to one of the buildings, drove quickly to the booth and jerked to a stop. Liam grabbed hold of Leila and pulled her to the side of the road and into the cover of some stunted trees.

They watched as a policeman got out of the car. He spoke to André and then signalled him to go and park. The Mercedes pulled forward and the police car followed it into the parking area. André got out of the Mercedes and the policeman led him inside the building.

Liam felt an odd mixture of emotions. It was terrible that André had been stopped but, on the other hand, he couldn't help feeling pleased that he had been proved right. The border police had been waiting for them. If they'd stayed in the car they would have been caught. He had followed his intuition and it had worked.

They waited for a quarter of an hour then a police van arrived from the French side of the border. A few minutes later André was led out to the van and driven away back towards France.

Leila wanted to stay and wait but Liam insisted that they had to carry on by themselves.

'Look, they were waiting for us,' he argued. 'Someone tipped them off. They'll have to let André go because they haven't got anything on him. But they'll follow him. If he's got any sense – and I think he has – he'll drive straight back to Paris and lead them away from us. We're better off on our own. Come on.'

He knew he was right and it must have shown because Leila simply fell in beside him as he turned and headed back towards Port-Bou.

He *was* right. He'd been right about not crossing the border. He'd been right about the boat. He'd been right about taking the bag out of the Mercedes. Somehow or other he was making all the right decisions. He could feel his confidence lifting. He was on a roll.

He felt so good that, as they came down into the town and he saw the truck standing on the quayside, he knew they would get a lift. The driver was loading trays of fish into the refrigerated rear of the truck and Liam went straight up to him and spoke to him in Spanish.

And, yes, he would give them a lift.

Where was he going? All the way to Madrid. It would be a long, slow journey and he hoped they didn't mind the smell of fish.

Yes, he could do with some help to finish loading – it would mean they'd be on the road even quicker.

The salt water from the crates stung the cracks in Liam's blistered hands but he didn't care. He was on a roll. It was as if all his senses were more alive than ever before and he was plugged in to everything around him.

He loaded the last crate and then happened to glance at Leila and saw her looking at him. She knew how he was feeling. She knew. And she felt like this nearly all the time. This intensity. This feeling of rightness. This being alive and in touch with things.

Then, like a combination lock clicking smoothly into place, he felt his senses move up another notch.

The stinging in his hands grew fiercer but that didn't matter. The light seemed to grow brighter, blindingly bright. The sounds from all around the harbour roared and pounded and sighed and slapped and creaked and screamed. Then everything faded away as he focused in on Leila. On her eyes that seemed to be looking straight through him.

It felt as if all barriers between them melted away and he was flooded with her. Flooded with Leila's mind and heart. Flooded with all she knew. Flooded with her whole spirit.

For an instant it was wonderful. Then a wild, falling terror burst inside him. He couldn't.

Couldn't stay.

He would die. Lose himself. Not be.

The muscles in his diaphragm jerked and his lungs gasped down a huge gulp of air. His eyes re-focused.

Like a door slamming, something inside him closed down and he was back in the harbour.

The sea was slapping against the harbour steps. A huge gull was pecking at a bloody mess of fish next to a pile of crates. The smell of diesel fumes hung in the air. The light was its usual brightness and the sounds were their usual loudness.

He looked at Leila and she smiled briefly then looked away as the lorry driver called them to get in the cab.

Liam knew she wouldn't say anything about it. And nor would he. There was nothing that could be said. Words didn't exist for it.

But it had happened. He was sure of that. He could still almost feel whatever it was. But it was going. Fading away so fast. Closing down. Almost gone already. Leaving what?'

Nothing.

Yes. A memory. Not even a picture memory. Just knowing.

Knowing what?

Knowing that he'd been somewhere. And it wasn't here.

Chapter Thirty

All morning the fish lorry trundled along at a steady sixty kilometres an hour. The sun beat down and the only relief was the breeze that flowed in through the cab windows. They stopped for a drink and a lunch of bread and cheese at about midday but it was so hot outside that they were happy to get moving again.

The air grew thicker and hotter in the afternoon and even the breeze felt like the blast from an oven. South of Zaragoza the driver pulled off the main road into a small lay-by next to a slow-moving river. There were some trees to give shade and they lay on the dry grass of the riverbank and dozed for a couple of hours.

Liam woke up with a start to find a large black fly biting his arm. He brushed it away and sat up. His mouth tasted bad and he knew that he had been having a horrible dream but he couldn't remember what it had been about.

They climbed back into the lorry and, as the sun sank lower, the breeze began to cool them off again. They stopped at nine o'clock for a meal at a roadside café and it was nearly midnight before they finally reached Madrid. The driver dropped them off near the fish market and Leila made a phone call to her contact. They walked into the centre of town and sat on the steps of a museum waiting for him to arrive.

The streets were still filled with noisy crowds taking advantage of the refreshing coolness of the night air. Whole families strolled past with babies and young children even though it was so late at night.

'What's the name of this guy who's coming?' Liam asked.

'Miguel Garcia,' Leila said. 'He's a friend of The Work – someone I can rely on.'

'Like Ahmad and that diplomat?'

'Yes.'

'How many of these "friends" are there?'

'All over the world? Thousands.'

'What's so special about them?' Liam asked, feeling a stab of resentment about these 'friends' she could rely on. What about him – couldn't she rely on him?

'I didn't say they were special. They're ordinary people who want to help Mankind fulfil its potential.'

'What the hell does that mean?' he snapped.

'Liam – it's nothing to be angry about or afraid of.'

'I'm not!' he said, but he was.

'What it means', Leila went on, ignoring him, 'is that human beings are evolving. They're changing. Usually it is a slow process but in certain people The Work can speed it up. It helps people to escape the lazy habits of the brain and learn how to think in a different way. And the new way of thinking can wake up things inside human beings who are ready for the change.'

'What things?'

'At the moment only five of our senses are awake – sight, hearing, touch, taste and smell – but for thousands of years other senses have been developing. When those senses wake up inside you, the whole way of understanding things is changed. It's like the difference between being blind and being able to see. It's like stepping out of the darkness into the light.'

Liam knew what she was talking about. It was what he had felt last night and early this morning. It was about being more alive. Being more in touch with everything. Knowing things that you couldn't know in the ordinary way – like knowing that they would be stopped if they tried to cross the border.

But what about the other stuff? Was it that too? He had glimpsed what it was like to enter someone else's mind. And the horror of it. The terror of feeling that he was about to disappear, lose himself, melt away and not be.

'It's powerful and it can be frightening,' Leila said and he knew she had heard his unspoken question. 'You have to get used to it. And I told you before, these things can only be fully woken up in people who can deal with it and who wouldn't misuse it.'

'And these thousands of "friends" – are they all like that?' Liam asked.

'Some of them. Others have only had glimpses – like you. They know that our ordinary senses can't tell us everything. They know there's something else and they want to learn more. Perhaps they'll be able to make the change, perhaps they won't. It is not enough just to want it, you have to be ready for it.'

'Don't they mind if they can't do it? I mean, aren't they jealous of people who can?' he asked, knowing that he was.

'They know that emotions like jealousy and impatience stop them learning, so they try to overcome them.'

It was a gentle put-down but he knew it was meant for him, so he didn't ask any more.

Bit by bit the streets emptied out as people finally began to drift home. The night air grew almost cold and they both pulled on sweatshirts to keep warm. A couple of young drunken men staggered by and called out something to Leila. Liam stood up and walked down the steps in case they started to cause trouble but they moved on and disappeared round the corner.

And then, at nearly three in the morning, a car pulled up in front of the museum and a man got out.

'Is that him?' Liam asked.

'I don't know,' Leila said.

The man was coming towards them. He was looking hard at them. Suddenly his hand went inside his jacket and Liam stood up quickly and put himself in front of Leila. If he had a gun . . .

The man pulled out a piece of paper and unfolded it. It was a photo. He glanced at it and then smiled up at them.

'Leila? Liam? I am Miguel Garcia. I am honoured to be able to help you.'

The first streaks of daylight were in the sky when they pulled into the small walled town of Sepudillo. They rattled through the narrow cobbled streets and out on to a large open space.

'Welcome to my house,' Miguel said as they got out of the car.

'You live here?' Liam said in disbelief, looking up at the walls of a small medieval castle.

'Yes.'

They crossed a wooden drawbridge and Miguel took a huge key out of his pocket and fitted it into the lock of the arched door. The door swung open and they stepped through into a courtyard.

Liam nudged Leila's arm as they watched Miguel locking the gate behind them. 'It'd take an army to get in! We'll be safe here.'

'I hope so,' Leila said.

But she didn't sound sure.

Chapter Thirty-one

Only about eighty people lived in Sepudillo but every day hundreds of tourists came to visit the ancient village. They strolled round the narrow streets looking at the old houses and then most of them took the guided visit to the castle.

Miguel Garcia was an architect and had bought the castle ten years earlier. In between running his successful business in Madrid he had set about restoring the run-down building. Now he and his wife, Antonia, lived in one wing of the castle and opened the rest of it to visitors as a way of paying for its upkeep.

There were still some parts of the castle that hadn't been renovated and Liam and Leila were happy to join in the work. They got up early and worked during the coolest part of the day: Liam helping the two carpenters who were rebuilding an old staircase, and Leila helping Antonia to whitewash walls.

By two o'clock in the afternoon the heat was so intense that everyone stopped work for the day. Leila usually went to her room to rest or read but Liam went down to a café and spent the afternoon with the carpenters. They were both over seventy and he could hardly understand a word of their rapid Spanish but they seemed to like him and he enjoyed playing cards with them. It was the two carpenters who showed him what they called The Killing Wall.

It was part of the high wall that ran round the village. This particular stretch was pitted with holes and the carpenters explained that over sixty people had been shot there during the Spanish Civil War. The village had been captured first by the Fascists and then by the Communists and each time the winning side had executed their enemies – men, women and children.

Liam couldn't follow the history very well but the wall fascinated him and he often went there to look at those bullet holes and think about the people who had died there. Sometimes he stood against the wall and tried to imagine what it would be like to know that you were just about to die.

How did those people face it? Did they beg for mercy? Did they cry as the firing squad took aim?

He imagined the terror. The feeling of helplessness as people got ready to take your life away from you.

Knowing that this was the last view you would ever see. The last glimpse of the sky. That this was your last breath. Your last heartbeat. Your last thought.

He imagined the bullets ripping into healthy bodies, smashing the life out of them. He looked at the ground and imagined the crumpled corpses and the blood.

So terrible. So final.

It was everything. Life was everything. To have it snatched away. All those things never done, never seen. And no coming back. No second chance. The end.

How could people do it to each other?

In the evenings Liam and Leila often walked out of a small back door in the castle wall and down the hill towards the river. The river had carved deep canyons into the rock and they walked along the top of them looking down at the water far below.

Vultures nested in small caves in the canyon walls and Liam and Leila watched them soaring on the thermals or gliding across the clifftops searching for food. One day Miguel came with them and showed them a narrow path down the cliff face to near the entrance to one of the caves where they could watch a vulture with her young. From then on they always made a point of going down that path to sit and wait for the spectacular sight of the huge bird flapping in and out of the cave to feed the chicks.

Liam loved these evening walks. The bare, savage countryside was unlike anything he'd ever known and the vultures were so wild and untamed. At sunset the huge red sun went down over the rocky plain, flaming the cliffs and the river with its glow. Then, suddenly, the night would come. The immense black sky filled up with astonishing clouds of dazzling stars, so bright and so pure.

Best of all, the walks gave him time to be alone with Leila. As they looked down at the river or sat waiting for the vulture to come she told him about the journeys she'd made with her father. She talked about the things she'd seen and the people she had met and it all came alive for him. But what he most liked to hear about was her home. When she spoke about her mother and the palace she had lived in, he could hear the love in her voice. He could almost smell the flowers in her garden and he could imagine the moon rising up from behind the Himalayas.

'I'd love to go there,' he said one evening.

'Perhaps you will. I know my parents will want to meet you. And you will walk in the mountains and think of me.'

'You'll be with me,' he said.

'The mountains are so high,' she went on. 'You feel closer to things up there. As if the barrier between this world and another dimension is thinner up there. It's as if you're nearer the gods.'

'What gods?'

'Whatever you want to call them. Gods. Advanced beings.'

'What, the ones you talk to?' he said, trying not to let it sound like a dig at her.

'I don't talk to them,' she said simply. 'I'm in touch with the people who do.'

'Oh yeah, like the whatsitsname of the Age?' And this time he couldn't help a little sarcastic edge creeping into his voice.

'The Keeper of the Age,' she said calmly, ignoring his tone. 'No, I'm in touch with a lower level than that.'

He could have gone on. He could have told her that he didn't believe all this stuff. But he didn't say anything. Part of him didn't believe it. Part of him thought the whole thing was stupid. But another part of him was beginning to believe everything she said.

He lay back on the ground and stared up at the night sky. The stars looked clearer and larger and more brilliant than ever. Easy to think about other dimensions when you looked at that immense beauty. Other dimensions. And gods.

And Liam was happy to leave it there. He didn't want a row with her. He just wanted to be here with her, lying on the dry ground and watching the amazing sparkle of the stars.

They did have a row one evening though, as they went past The Killing Wall on their way back from one of their walks. Liam pointed out the trace of the bullets – dark holes in the moonlit wall – and told her all his thoughts about the terror of being killed like that.

'Dying isn't so terrible,' she said.

'How do you know?' he snapped, angry that he had poured out all his secret fears for nothing.

She just shrugged and it made his temper rise. He *knew*. He'd seen Gran dead. He'd seen Dr Prior dead. What had they been? Dead meat. Nothing.

'How do you know?' he asked again, his voice rising with anger. 'Life's everything. It's all there is. A bit of life and then you're dead. That's all. And this lot had it smashed out of them.'

'Dying is not so terrible. And sometimes there are things worth dying for. Things you must die for,' Leila said.

'No!' he shouted, and for no good reason his eyes began to fill with tears. He had to look away towards the lights of the castle.

'Life isn't all there is,' she went on. 'Not this life. This life is only what our body knows. What our senses tell us. But our senses are so limited – they can't know everything. Our senses can't detect other dimensions but they are there.'

'How do you know if you can't detect them?' he growled, fighting back the tears.

'I mean that our ordinary senses can't detect them. But you've felt other senses stirring inside you, most people have. People call it all sorts of things – intuition, ESP. It's just about being more awake. You know what I mean. You don't just believe your eyes or your ears, Liam. You know there's more than that.'

'I don't!' he choked. 'It stinks! It just bloody stinks!'

The pain was squeezing his heart and he felt like falling to the ground and letting all his misery pour out but he forced himself to walk away across the dusty square towards the castle.

When he got to the gate he looked back and saw Leila still standing there, her arms slightly lifted to the side and her head raised towards the sky.

He went straight to his room and locked the door in case she tried to come in and talk to him again. But she didn't. He got into bed and found that all his anger and pain had gone. He lay quietly and calmly in the dark.

A thought came to him as he lay there and he smiled to himself. Leila was worth dying for.

Chapter Thirty-two

The stay in Sepudillo was the best of times for Liam. He liked the village. He liked his small bedroom with its white-painted walls and wooden floor and its view out over the plain towards the distant mountains. He liked the bright heat outside and the cool of the thick-walled castle. He liked the hard rebuilding work with the two carpenters. He liked the time he could spend with Leila. And he liked Miguel and Antonia Garcia.

Miguel and Antonia didn't have children of their own and they seemed delighted to have someone to look after. They obviously adored Leila but they treated her rather respectfully. With Liam, though, they were much less formal. Antonia was always trying to make him eat more.

'You are a very handsome boy, Liam, but too thin. You must eat!' she kept saying, and she loaded his plate with extra food.

She fussed about his clothes and took him to the nearest big town to buy some T-shirts and some shorts because she thought he looked too hot in jeans and ordinary shirts. She even made him go to the barber while they were in town to tidy up his hair that had been growing strangely since it had been singed in the fire.

'There! Much better,' she beamed when he came out with his hair cut really short. 'Now people can see your eyes instead of all that hair hanging down. Let me look. Yes, they are beautiful eyes, kind and intelligent. Ah yes, and I like it when you smile like that – sometimes your face is too solemn, too sad. You must smile more!'

It was easy to smile with her. She was lively and funny and she had so much energy and enthusiasm. But she could be quiet too, and easy to talk to. One very hot afternoon he was helping her prepare the evening meal in the large kitchen. The doors were open to create a cooling draught. She was peeling vegetables and he was washing the lettuce and tomatoes in a bowl of cold water. He mentioned his half-sister, Danielle, and then suddenly found himself pouring out all the details about his mother, about Mr Watling, about Gran. Things he'd never told anyone, not even Leila. Everything.

When he finished, he realized that his hands were still in the bowl and that they were numb from the cold water. There was silence behind him and he wondered if Antonia had gone. Before he could turn to look, she put her arms round him and held on to him tightly. She kissed the back of his head. Then she let go and they went on with their work. She didn't ask questions or say anything.

Liam saw less of Miguel because he was away most days at his office in Madrid but he liked him just as much. They often played tennis together on a dusty court just outside the village or drove in Miguel's battered old military jeep to go fishing in a remote lake. Miguel joked and laughed and talked about unimportant things but Liam felt calmer and stronger when he spent time with him.

The only time Miguel ever talked directly about something important was early one Sunday morning when they were fishing at the lake. The water was so still that the reflection of the mountains looked almost as real as the mountains themselves. Neither of them had spoken for about ten minutes.

Then Miguel suddenly turned and said, 'You must learn patience, Liam. The Work operates on a very long timescale. Sometimes it plants a seed that will only grow after hundreds of years. Sometimes things look as if they have failed but really they have succeeded. You must remember that when you think about Leila.'

Liam didn't really understand why Miguel had said it but he didn't have a chance to ask because there was a tug at his line and he started battling with a large pike that he'd caught. In the end the pike broke the line and swam away into the black depths of the lake just when he was about to land it.

Liam would have liked to stay at Sepudillo for ever. The castle began to feel like home. Then, three months after they arrived, Miguel came back from Madrid with an English magazine that he had seen in a shop.

There was an article about the huge number of children and teenagers who went missing every year and it used Liam and Leila as an example. It said that they had stayed in Paris and then probably crossed the border into Spain but, unlike the other articles, there was no suggestion that they were being hunted for murder. Instead, it seemed more concerned about their safety.

They both read the article sitting at the kitchen table then Leila looked up at Miguel and said, 'It's nearly time.'

He nodded and his face looked worn and unhappy.

Ten days later Miguel brought home a Spanish magazine which carried a translation of the same article. Then three days after that he showed them a small item in a Spanish newspaper. The lorry driver from Port-Bou had come forward to talk to the police about giving a lift to two people who resembled Liam and Leila.

'Why?' Liam demanded. 'Why's it all starting up again? Why can't they leave us alone?'

Leila looked at him but she didn't say anything.

After feeling so relaxed and safe, they had to be careful again. They stopped going out into the village and even stayed in their rooms when there were tourists looking round the castle in case anyone recognized them. Even so, Liam still hoped that the publicity would die down and they would be able to stay in Sepudillo.

Then, one Sunday morning, he was looking out of a window at a group of tourists who were waiting outside the castle. He was casually watching the guide selling the tickets for the next tour when his heart jerked in shock.

He had recognized one of the faces in the crowd.

Chapter Thirty-three

Liam had only just glimpsed the man before he'd turned away. Now he stared at the man's back, hoping it was a mistake.

Perhaps he was imagining things. Perhaps it was only a vague resemblance. But the fat body and the blond hair looked terribly familiar. It looked like the driver from that night outside Dr Prior's house.

'Turn round,' Liam whispered through clenched teeth. 'Turn round!'

Then Liam saw the brown-skinned man walking towards the group from the direction of the car park. And this time there was no doubt. It was Nayeem.

He walked up to the driver and said something. The two men glanced up at the castle walls as they followed the rest of the tourists through the door into the courtyard. Liam pulled back from the window then charged out of the room and down the stairs.

Leila and Antonia were sitting at the kitchen table and they looked up in surprise as he burst in.

'What is it?' Antonia asked.

'It's the guys who killed Doctor Prior,' Liam shouted as he ran to the window and looked out.

The group of tourists was following the guide across the courtyard but the two men weren't going with them. They had stopped and were looking towards the kitchen door.

Liam rushed to the door and locked it.

'We've got to get out of here. Where's Miguel?'

'In the village somewhere,' Antonia said. 'We can go and find him.'

'No! We'll be an easy target out on the streets. You go – they're not looking for you. We'll go and hide down by the river. Tell Miguel to meet us there.'

Liam looked out of the window again. The men were walking towards the kitchen door.

'Quick, Antonia – go!'

Antonia ran out into the hall and they heard her slam the front door behind her.

'Come on, we'll go this way,' Liam said, pulling Leila in the other direction.

'What about our things?' Leila asked.

'We haven't got time. Quick!'

At the top of the steps to the cellar they stopped and looked back towards the kitchen. The door handle was rattling as the men tried to get in. Then there was a crash of glass as one of them smashed the window.

Liam closed the cellar door and slid the two bolts across. It would take the men some time to break it open.

They ran down the stairs to the cellar and then across to the small back door. The bright sunlight blinded them as they opened the door and dashed out on to the path below the castle walls.

The heat bounced off the dusty plain as they fled towards the river. There was no cover out here and nowhere to hide until they got to the canyon. Liam glanced back towards the castle and stumbled as his foot twisted on a stone. He staggered and nearly fell but Leila caught him by the wrist and steadied him. She slid her hand down into his and they raced towards the river together.

The hot dry air was burning their lungs by the time they reached the lip of the canyon. They ran along the edge, heading for the narrow path down to the river. If they could just get there without being seen . . .

When they reached the path Liam looked back towards the castle and his heart sank. Two figures were coming

134

out of the cellar door. They stopped for a moment then one of them pointed in their direction and they began running again.

'They've seen us,' he panted. 'Come on!'

They started down the steep path, slipping and sliding on the loose stones.

'We'll have to swim for it,' Leila gasped. 'Nowhere to hide.'

Liam's mind was racing. They would go all the way down to the small beach at the bottom and into the water. The current was strong there and just a little way downstream it got faster, much faster. The rapids would carry them a long way in a short time but it was dangerous. Maybe they would be lucky and find a branch or a log to hang on to.

But even as he thought it he knew they wouldn't be lucky. They wouldn't find a log or a branch. And he had a swift picture of the two of them being swept headlong towards the sharp rocks. And he knew it wasn't just a fear. It was what was going to happen.

He pulled on Leila's hand and they skidded to a stop.

'We can't go down there – we'll be trapped.'

'The river – ' Leila began.

'No!' he shouted, cutting her short. 'No. I saw . . . We can't.'

He turned and pulled her uphill.

'No, Liam. They'll be coming down.'

'Just follow me,' he ordered.

Exactly like the time at the crossing of the frontier, he felt as if he couldn't make a bad decision. He knew it was wrong to go to the river. And he knew it was right to head uphill.

They toiled up the slope and suddenly came to the spot where they had sat and watched the vulture flying in and out to its nest in the cave.

'The cave,' he said. 'We'll hide in the cave.'

'It's too obvious,' Leila said.

She was right. It was obvious. But, as he stared at the cave, he felt certain that they had to hide there. At any moment the two men would reach the path. There was no choice.

'Come on,' he said and began scrambling up the slope to the mouth of the cave.

He reached the entrance and placed his hands on the rock and hauled himself up. Then he turned round and held out his hand. Leila hesitated then reached up and took it. He braced himself and pulled her up.

It was dark inside and they shuffled forward, not sure where they were putting their feet. There was a hissing sound and then a scrabbling noise. Liam squinted his eyes and saw a young vulture standing on a pile of branches staring at them in terror.

He took a step forward and the vulture began flapping its wings in panic and dashing from side to side of the cave.

'Sshh!' Leila said softly. 'Ssshh. It's all right. It's all right.'

The vulture stopped moving and looked at her. She tiptoed forward and the vulture let her go past. Liam followed.

The roof of the cave sloped down and they bent double and kept going until they could go no further. They got on their hands and knees and squeezed themselves against the back wall and waited.

Liam's heart was beating fast and he could feel Leila's body rocking with the pulse of her blood. They stared at the cave entrance with the young vulture's head and body silhouetted against the light.

There was the sound of sliding footsteps. An indistinct voice. Then silence.

Liam and Leila stopped breathing.

The footsteps came again and they knew that the men were heading towards the cave. They heard a scrambling noise then the top of Nayeem's head came into view. He put his hands on the flat rock of the entrance and lifted himself up to look into the cave.

They froze.

He seemed to be staring straight at them.

'Can't see,' he said. 'Give me a push up.'

'Come on, we're wasting time. They're down at the river,' the driver said.

'Shut up and let me check! Push!' Nayeem ordered. Then he braced his hands on the rock and started to haul himself up into the cave.

Liam got ready. He had made a mistake. His instinct had let him down and they were trapped. There was just one thing he could do – charge at Nayeem and hope to knock him backwards out of the cave. If he ran full tilt and went over the edge with him they might just catch the driver and all three of them would crash down the side of the canyon towards the river. It was the only hope, the only way of giving Leila a chance to escape.

Liam took a deep breath and tensed his muscles for the dash forward.

There was a loud shrieking noise and something huge shot past the entrance of the cave.

It was the female vulture.

Nayeem raised his hand to protect his head and almost slipped backwards but he managed to grab hold of the rock at the side of the cave and start to haul himself up again.

The young vulture let out a hiss and began beating its wings and squealing. Nayeem stopped, startled by this strange noise from inside the cave.

Then, framed in the circle of the cave entrance, Liam saw the female vulture come back into view. She wheeled round over the canyon and flapped urgently towards her nest.

The noise of her high-pitched cry of 'Kweee, Kweee' echoed round the rocks.

Nayeem jerked his head round, took one look at the approaching vulture, and called out, 'Let go! Let me down!'

He disappeared from view and then the whole entrance of the cave was darkened by the body and wings of the vulture as she glided inside. Still uttering her savage cry, she turned with her wings outstretched and strutted back to the mouth of the cave, defying the enemy to come near her young.

There were curses from below and then the sound of rolling rocks as the two men scrambled down towards the path again.

'They're going down to the river,' Liam whispered. 'We'll give them time to get down there and then we'll go.'

It was a great temptation to move at once but he forced himself to count slowly to two hundred.

'OK,' he said and they started to crawl forward.

The young vulture immediately began to shriek and flap its wings and the mother turned round and hopped back into the cave. Liam had a sudden panic as he imagined the huge bird charging at them. On their hands and knees like this, her huge, sharp beak would come straight for their eyes.

'Ssh,' Leila said softly. 'Ssh.'

The vultures stood still.

Leila kept moving forward until she could stand up. The two vultures watched her silently. She held out her hands and moved them gently and the birds stared at them as if hypnotized.

'Ssh. It's all right,' she said and then made a high-pitched drone at the back of her throat and a rapid clicking sound with her tongue.

The birds moved back against the wall, the mother pushing her large chick with her body.

Leila beckoned to Liam and he crawled forward until he could stand. He went past Leila and jumped out of the cave. A moment later she joined him and they skidded down the short slope and on to the path. They glanced down to the bottom of the canyon. Nayeem and the driver were scrambling over the large boulders near the beach.

Then, from up above, came the loud hooting of a car horn. The men heard it too, and looked up and saw them.

'Come on!' Liam shouted and began racing up the path, followed by Leila.

When they reached the top he glanced down and saw that the men had run across the beach and were scrambling back on to the path.

There was another blast from the horn and he turned and saw Miguel's battered old jeep bumping away from them across the plain. He grabbed Leila's hand and they ran after him, screaming Miguel's name.

The jeep continued to speed away from them then suddenly it slowed. Miguel began blaring on the horn again and started to turn the jeep on a long sweep of the plain. He was halfway round the arc when he saw them.

He revved the engine and the jeep raced back towards them. It skidded to a stop in a cloud of dust and Miguel pulled Leila on to the front seat with him. Liam jumped on to the open back and they were off, jolting across the rocky plain.

Great plumes of dust shot out from the rear wheels and Liam couldn't see much, but when the jeep suddenly lurched to the right to avoid a rock he saw the two men. They had reached the top of the path and were watching the jeep roar away from them.

He saw them both lean forward and put their hands on their knees in exhaustion. They had given up the chase.

Chapter Thirty-four

It was too risky to go back to the castle to collect their things and Miguel said that Antonia was safe with friends in the village so they headed away from Sepudillo. They drove across the rocky plain for ten minutes until they came to the main road. They bumped across a ditch and up the slope on to the tarmac then turned right towards Madrid.

The dusty old jeep seemed to crawl along the highway to the city and Liam kept checking the cars that roared past them from the direction of Sepudillo. Then, at last, they were turning left and right in the maze of crowded city streets in Madrid and he felt sure they hadn't been followed.

They stopped at Miguel's bank and he drew out as much money as he could from the automatic till. Then they went to his office and waited while he rang various people to ask if he could borrow money.

It was nearly dark by the time they finished driving round the city to pick up the money from his friends.

'Nobody carries much cash nowadays but this lot should last you a couple of months at least,' he said as he got back into the car after the last stop. 'I can pay your train fares with my credit card and you'll be able to live cheaply in Morocco.'

'But we haven't got our passports,' Liam pointed out. 'You'll have to send them to us.'

'That means phoning me with your address. It's too dangerous – you never know who's listening to phone calls or tracing mail. Your best hope is to find someone who'll smuggle you across.'

He drove them to the station and bought tickets for an overnight train to Seville and then onwards to Cadiz.

Standing in the hot station surrounded by large palm trees growing in tubs, Miguel said goodbye to them.

He hugged Liam.

'Remember us. We're always here if you need us. When you're ready, yes?'

Liam nodded and looked away to where their train was waiting. It hurt to say goodbye. He wanted to stay.

Miguel took Leila's hand and kissed it then bowed his head. She laid her hand on the top of his head for a couple of moments.

'Don't be afraid for me, Miguel,' she said as she took her hand away. 'It will be easy. Tell Antonia. I know she worries about it.'

'I will. So . . . Travel well.'

He hardly seemed able to drag his eyes from Leila's face but finally he turned away. They watched him as he rode the escalator up to the street. He waved and disappeared.

Miguel had booked a first-class sleeping compartment for them and it was good to be able to crash out on their bunks and let the rattling of the train rock them to sleep.

They both woke early and sat at the window watching the dry valleys and hills roll by in the grey, pearly dawn. Mists lay across rivers and streams and olive groves. Cattle browsed on the heat-scorched grass. They passed scrubby white houses where people were living their hard lives miles from anyone else.

That young boy leading a donkey down a dusty track; that woman feeding chickens; that farmer at work in his maize field; that girl walking on the river bank. Liam clattered past them in the train and some of them looked up to watch him go by.

The world was so big. There were so many people living on it. Living lives so different from his. It made him feel small but it also made him feel free. His life didn't have to be like it used to be. He could choose.

They had breakfast of coffee and churros in a small café opposite the station in Seville then they spent the morning shopping for clothes. Leila only bought a few essential things for herself but she kept picking out shirts and sweaters and holding them up against him.

'Oh, that looks great, Liam – you've got to get it. It'll go great with those trousers we bought.'

'I've got enough!'

'No, you haven't – I want you to look nice. Come on, we'll buy it.'

They bought a travel bag and her new clothes only took up a small corner, while his stuff filled the rest of it.

'I've got what I need,' she said. 'Stop fussing.'

The train from Seville was filled with young sailors from the Spanish Navy who had been on leave for the weekend and were returning to their ships. Liam and Leila couldn't get a seat and they stood in the crowded corridor with the sailors who drank beers and laughed and shouted and teased and jostled each other all the way to Cadiz. A couple of them kept smiling at Leila and eventually one of them offered to buy her a beer but she put her arm round Liam's shoulder and told them that her boyfriend would be jealous.

The sailor grinned at Liam and said, 'Qué afortunado eres!'

Liam smiled back and knew that he was 'afortunado': lucky to have Leila's arm round him, lucky to be on this strange journey with her, lucky to have her say he was her boyfriend even if it wasn't true.

When they arrived in Cadiz they wandered down to the port and looked southwards. Somewhere across the sea, hidden in the haze, lay Africa.

Chapter Thirty-five

They found a cheap hotel near the fish market in Cadiz. From dawn to dark the narrow streets round the market rumbled and heaved with trolleys and lorries while fishermen and traders argued and bargained among the crates of fish and the barrels of ice. Women sat at bloody slabs, gutting the fish. The drainage channels ran with melted ice and blood and fish scales. The autumn sun was still hot and by midday the buzz of flies and the stench of the fish was unbearable.

Liam and Leila spent the afternoons out on the long beach south of the harbour. The breeze was fresh and clean and they could walk for hours along the empty sand. They didn't have swimsuits but they often just went into the warm water in their shorts and tops and then let the sun and breeze dry them as they went on walking.

In the evenings Liam went down to the harbour on his own. He went into cafés and listened to the fishermen as they drank and chatted before their night's fishing. He followed them down to the quay and watched as they prepared their boats, cast off, and sailed out into the darkness. Then he got up early in the morning and watched as they sailed back and unloaded their night's catch.

On the fifth morning, he was sitting on the dockside watching the fleet come in. One of the boats drew up to the wall and the fisherman smiled and threw a rope to him.

Liam caught the end and tied it to one of the iron rings along the quayside.

'Gracias,' the man said.

'Can I help?' Liam asked in Spanish and then mimed lifting a crate in case the man hadn't understood his accent.

The fisherman shrugged as if he couldn't care less but he handed a crate of fish up. Liam took it and put it down on the edge of the quay then reached for another.

Liam stacked the crates in piles of six just as he'd seen the men do every morning. By the time the whole catch had been unloaded there were eight neatly stacked piles. The fisherman climbed up from the boat and looked along the quay at his rivals who were still struggling to unload their catches. He grinned at Liam.

'Gracias,' he said and slipped a trolley under one of the piles of boxes and began wheeling it along the cobbled street to the market.

Liam grabbed another trolley, slid it under the next pile of boxes, and hurried after the fisherman. They arrived at the market house together.

One of the buyers stepped up and looked at the twelve crates. He picked up one of the fish and examined it.

'How many crates?' he asked.

'Forty-eight,' the fisherman said.

'OK,' the buyer said and scribbled a price on a piece of paper on his clipboard.

The fisherman looked at the figure then spat on his hand and held it out. The buyer spat on his own hand then smacked it against the fisherman's.

'The lorry leaves in ten minutes,' the buyer said.

Liam and the fisherman ran backwards and forwards fetching the other thirty-six crates. By the time they had finished, the other men were only just arriving with their catches. The fisherman waved his handful of notes at them and laughed then put his arm round Liam's shoulder and pulled him to the café across the road. He bought two beers and they clinked bottles.

'My name is Carlos,' he said.

'Liam.'

They shook hands then stood in the doorway drinking their beer and watching the other fishermen carrying their fish and trying to find a buyer. When he finished his bottle, Liam said he had to go. Carlos held out some money.

'No. It's OK,' Liam said.

The next morning he waited on the quayside and helped Carlos unload his catch as soon as the boat was tied up. It was a smaller haul, only thirty-seven crates, but they were first at the market and Carlos got a good price. They went to the café for a beer and, again, Liam refused the offer of money.

'I want to go to Morocco,' he said.

Carlos jerked his head in the direction of the port and said, 'Ferry.'

'No passport,' Liam said softly.

Carlos grimaced and shrugged, 'Impossible.'

'I can pay.'

He half-pulled a wad of notes out of his jeans pocket.

Carlos looked at the money and then up at Liam. He narrowed his eyes and repeated, 'Impossible.'

'OK,' Liam said. He drank up his beer and waved to Carlos. 'See you tomorrow.'

When the boat chugged into harbour the next morning, Liam was waiting on the quayside and it was obvious Carlos hadn't expected him to be there.

'You work?' Carlos asked.

'I work,' Liam said and bent down to take the first crate.

There were fifty-one crates but they were still the first to arrive at the market and again Carlos got the top price of the day.

'You take some money,' Carlos said in the café afterwards and tried to push some notes into Liam's hand.

'No, I don't want money. I want to go to Morocco.'

Carlos lit a cigarette and spat through the doorway on to the pavement.

'Moroccans come here. You don't want to go there,' Carlos said in a low voice.

'I do. You can take us.'

'Us?'

'Me and a girl.'

'A girl? No, no – it's impossible.'

'I'll pay.'

'Impossible.'

'OK. You don't take me to Morocco,' Liam said walking to the door. He turned and smiled. 'I still help you.'

The following morning he was waiting on the quay when Carlos sailed back after his night's fishing. Carlos handed him the crates one after the other but he didn't look Liam in the eye. At the end of their usual race to the market house, they were walking to the café when Carlos took Liam's arm and pulled him into a side alley.

'Tomorrow night. I'll take you. We meet a Moroccan boat. They'll take you. You pay now.'

'How much?' Liam asked, pulling the wad of notes from his pocket.

'This,' Carlos said, grabbing the notes.

'That's too much!' Liam said. It was nearly half of all their money.

'I have to pay the police,' Carlos said. 'They don't look, they don't see.'

'OK,' Liam said. 'OK.'

'Eight o'clock tomorrow night,' Carlos whispered then hurried away down the alley.

Liam thought that Leila would be pleased when he told her but she just nodded and looked out of the window.

'What's up?' he asked. 'It's good, isn't it? We're going to Morocco. That's what you want, isn't it?'

'It's not what I want, it's what I've got to do. I'd rather stay here or go somewhere else. But I can't. I can't.'

There was a long silence while she stared out of the window. Liam didn't know what to do. Her voice sounded so sad and he couldn't think of anything to say to cheer her up.

Then suddenly she seemed to make up her mind about something. She lifted her shoulders and turned round.

'I'm sorry,' she said. 'I'm being stupid. Wasting time being miserable.'

She made a silly face then flashed a beautiful smile at him.

'Come on, let's celebrate our last night in Europe. Let's have a barbecue on the beach! I'll go and buy the things we need – it'll be great.'

At half-past seven they went out on to the beach and walked away from the harbour until they came to the sand dunes. Liam collected bits of driftwood and lit the fire while Leila prepared the food. As the sun went down she stuffed some fish with fresh herbs and slices of lemon then wrapped them in foil and placed them in the heart of the flames.

'See, I've thought of everything,' Leila said, pulling a small portable radio from her bag.

She tuned the radio to a station that was playing dance music and she began moving to the beat. Liam joined in but she started doing wild steps and funny jumps and he laughed so much that he fell over and just lay there watching her mucking around.

Then they sat and ate the fish with a salad and warm bread. Everything was great, especially the fish.

'It's the best I've ever tasted,' Liam said.

'Everything tastes better outdoors.'

'Yeah, but putting the herbs and lemon in with the fish was brilliant. You're an ace cook.'

'Thanks,' Leila said and leaned over and gave him a quick kiss on his cheek. 'Thanks for being here.'

When they finished eating they wandered along the beach letting the warm sea roll over their feet as they watched the moon begin to rise.

The fire was just a pile of glowing embers by the time they got back. Leila turned the radio on again and tuned it to a station that was playing quieter music. She put her arms round Liam and held on to him as they swayed backwards and forwards to the music.

Her head was pressed against Liam's chest and he felt sure she must be able to hear the way his heart was knocking loudly with happiness. He closed his eyes and listened to the soft music and the shushing of the waves on the sand. All he could feel was her body, warm against his.

He wanted to tell her he loved her but he couldn't say the words. He just hoped that she knew.

Chapter Thirty-six

Liam half expected Carlos not to turn up, but the boat was in the usual place when he and Leila arrived on the quay. He called softly and Carlos came out of the cabin on to the deck. The fisherman quickly glanced up and down the dock then put out his hand and helped them aboard.

'In the cabin,' he said.

They went down the four steps to the cabin. It was a tiny, stuffy space with a jumble of nets and charts and tins of food on the floor.

'You sit there,' Carlos said, pointing to a small table in the corner.

He turned off the gas lamp, went out on to the deck and closed the door. They sat in the darkness and heard the engine start. The boat began to throb as it moved out of Cadiz harbour.

Half an hour out to sea, the door opened and Carlos called them out on deck. They were chugging down the coast and the lights of Cadiz were already a long way behind them. There was hardly any wind but there was a heavy swell and the small boat swayed and rocked as the waves passed under her. They sat on the roof of the cabin and looked across the moonlit sea towards the dark land. From time to time car headlights flashed on the coastal roads and little clusters of lights showed where there was a village.

Four hours out of Cadiz, the sea suddenly became rougher and the boat bucked up and down as waves slapped her sides. Spray shot from the bows and splattered them.

'The Mediterranean,' Carlos shouted, pointing to the left. He then pointed to the right, 'The Atlantic.' He brought his hands together with a loud crash to show the meeting of the two currents. 'Boom!'

He laughed as a particularly large wave slammed into the boat and made her judder.

'Over there,' he added, pointing to a glow in the night sky. 'Tangier. Morocco. Africa.'

In less than an hour the glow from Tangier was behind them and the sea was calmer again.

Carlos spoke into the radio and a crackly reply came back.

'My Moroccan friend,' he explained and then concentrated on scanning the horizon.

He made two more calls on the radio and then they saw the lights of another boat heading out from the coast. Carlos picked up a flashlight and waved it in a circle. Someone on board the other boat repeated the signal.

Carlos eased back on the throttle and the two boats moved slowly towards each other until they bumped gently. The man from the Moroccan boat leaned over and grabbed hold of the side of their boat.

'Go!' Carlos said, throwing their bag over on to the Moroccan boat. Liam held out his hand to say farewell but the Spaniard looked away.

Liam climbed across on to the Moroccan boat and then helped Leila on board. She had barely set foot on deck when Carlos dashed back to the wheel. He revved the throttle and powered away, leaving the Moroccan boat rocking in his wake. They watched him go for a few seconds and then turned to find themselves standing in front of a swarthy man with a huge scar that ran from his forehead, down across a milky blind eye, and on to his cheek. He held out his hand and rubbed his thumb across the tips of his fingers.

'L'argent,' he said.

'We've paid money. To Carlos,' Liam said, pointing over his shoulder to the departing boat. 'We've paid him.'

'L'argent,' the man repeated.

'Carlos . . .' Liam began and then stepped back as the man raised his other hand and showed the long stiletto knife he was holding.

Liam looked at Leila and shrugged defeat. He bent down and opened up the side pocket of the travel bag and took out the money that was there. He started peeling some notes away but the man snatched the whole roll out of his hand.

There was no point in arguing so Liam picked up the bag and walked over to the side of the boat. Leila followed and they sat side by side on the bag. The man grinned and went into the little wheelhouse. The engine coughed into life and they began heading towards the coast.

Half an hour later they saw lights and they could just make out the shape of a walled town on the top of rocks that rose out of the sea. They chugged along past the town and then swung into a harbour guarded by a concrete breakwater with strange triangular shapes along the top.

The Moroccan cut the engine and the boat glided past other fishing boats and some luxurious-looking yachts. It bumped against the quay and the man came out of the wheelhouse. He picked up their bag, threw it ashore, and clicked his fingers and pointed to show that they should follow. Liam jumped first then he bent and held the boat steady while Leila stepped on to the quay.

The Moroccan pushed off with his foot and darted into the wheelhouse. The engine puttered and the boat began backing out of the harbour.

Liam suddenly felt light-hearted and afraid at the same time.

'Well, you wanted to come to Morocco,' he said. 'Here we are.'

'Yes,' Leila said quietly. 'Here we are.'

Chapter Thirty-seven

They found a sheltered corner against the walls of the old town and sat down to wait for the dawn. Leila was very quiet and withdrawn and Liam wondered if she was worried about the money. He had been going to keep the surprise until later but he wanted to cheer her up so he took off his shoes and showed her all the notes that he had hidden there.

'They probably stink,' he laughed. 'And they hurt like hell to walk on. But at least that bloke didn't get the lot. Brilliant, eh?'

Leila nodded then stared off into the distance again, her face looking sadder than Liam had ever seen it. It made his heart clench with pain to see her like that but he didn't know what to say or do. He started humming a tune then stopped, embarrassed. He thought of lots of things to say but they all seemed stupid. He wanted to put his arm round her and just hold her tight until she stopped being sad but he didn't dare. Instead, he got up and strolled across the big dusty square in front of the walls.

Leila's mood had changed as soon as they had landed. She had suddenly become remote and cold. And yet she ought to be pleased. They had made it. For six months Morocco had been their destination. He could remember that moment, standing in the tube station in London, when she had first mentioned the name. It had seemed impossible then – just the name of a faraway place he couldn't even imagine. And yet here they were. She ought to be happy. Their journey was over.

And suddenly he realized that he had always thought of Morocco as the end. They would arrive and all the danger and worry would be over. As if all this time he had expected someone would be here to welcome them and say, 'Well done – mission completed.' He had never actually thought beyond getting here. But was it all over? Were they safe now? Had the enemy given up?

He looked back to where Leila was sitting, hunched down with her head on her knees. Was her destiny still tied up with the Keeper of the Age like she had said? If it was, then the danger would never be over. He would have to ask her, but not yet.

The sky was getting lighter and suddenly there were signs of life. A battered old van went by in the direction of the harbour. Someone opened the shutters of a small window at the top of a house inside the town wall. A man in a brown woollen robe came down the road, leading a donkey. He stopped under a palm tree at the edge of the square and began unloading things from the donkey and laying them out on the ground. Liam wandered across and saw that they were simple clay pots. The man looked up and said something in Arabic then held up one of the pots.

'No, no thanks. Merci, non,' Liam said, suddenly feeling a bit panicky at not being able to speak the language.

He walked quickly back towards Leila. As he got closer he could see that she was still hunched forward in the same position. She didn't want him. She was cutting herself off from him. He'd helped her to get here and she hadn't even thanked him. He changed direction and went and sat down further along the wall.

There were other people coming down the road now – men and women. Some were leading donkeys laden with crates, others were carrying baskets of vegetables and fruit. When they reached the square they looked for a spare space and then simply put their goods down on the ground. A market was taking shape in front of his eyes.

Soon there were customers strolling up and down, peering at the goods. The air filled up with the noise of haggling voices. Liam watched the growing activity for nearly half an hour and then suddenly felt drawn to look across at Leila. She was sitting up, looking straight at him. She smiled and he could see that her mood had changed. He walked towards her and sat down.

'It's a market,' he said, for something to say.

She nodded.

'I'm sorry,' she said. 'I just suddenly felt . . . scared . . . and down.'

'It's OK,' he replied. His voice was cool – as if he hadn't been upset, as if he'd hardly noticed anything.

'Anyway,' she said and she suddenly had a mischievous smile on her face, 'our mission isn't completed yet. We've got to get to Fez.'

He looked at her and grinned and blushed. She knew what he'd been thinking. He couldn't hide anything from her.

They had breakfast in a café – a bowl of yoghurt with honey and a jug of freshly squeezed orange juice – and watched the bustle of the market. Leila spoke Arabic to the woman running the café and asked her how they could get to Fez. She told them to take a taxi a short way down the coast to a place called Larache and then catch a bus from there. Liam couldn't understand a word but the woman kept stopping and smiling at him while Leila translated. The woman even agreed to take their Spanish money and change it for Moroccan dirham.

'She says she will give us the best rate,' Leila translated.

Liam smiled his gratitude at the woman and said, 'Merci.'

But then Leila added, 'In fact, she'll give us a bad rate and she's decided to overcharge us for breakfast. But it doesn't matter – she's poor and her family needs all the money she can get.'

'How do you know all that?' Liam asked.

Leila shrugged.

As they were crossing the market place Leila stopped at a stall selling clothes and picked up a green caftan with a hood. She held it up in front of her and asked Liam how she looked.

'Beautiful,' he said – and it was true. 'Buy it.'

'No. There's no . . . It's a waste,' she said, putting it down.

'Go on, buy it,' Liam said but she was already walking towards the line of taxis that stood at the edge of the market. She went along asking for Larache until one of the drivers nodded and jerked his thumb to show they should get in.

'Why's he not going?' Liam asked after they had been sitting there for a minute.

'It's a communal taxi – we're waiting for other people who want to go to Larache.'

Five minutes later there was still nobody else so Liam said, 'Wait there – don't let him go!' Then he jumped out of the taxi and ran back to the stall.

'How much?' he said to the owner, holding up the caftan.

The man said something in Arabic so Liam took a Moroccan banknote from his pocket and held it up. The man shook his head and pointed to the note and held up five fingers. Liam shook his head and held up the note again. The man shook his head and held up three fingers. Liam put the caftan down and turned away.

He had only taken a few paces when the man called again – he was holding up the caftan and running his hand across it to show how beautiful it was. Liam took out another note and held them both up. The man nodded. Liam handed him the two notes, took the caftan, and ran back to the taxi.

'You'll look great in it!' he said, giving the caftan to Leila.

'Oh Liam, it's lovely,' she said. 'It's lovely. Thanks.'

She was just unfolding it when two large women in black robes and veils opened the taxi door and squeezed in next to her. They had baskets of shopping with them and by the time they were installed they took up nearly all of the back seat and Liam and Leila were crushed together in the corner.

The taxi inched forward until it broke through the crowds, then the driver put his foot down and they shot forward. An old man was crossing the road leading a donkey and a camel. The driver hooted his horn and only just missed hitting them. There were screams and laughter from the two large women as the taxi swerved back on course.

Liam was too squashed to turn and look fully at Leila but he could see her hand stroking the green material of the caftan. He glanced sideways and saw a tear running down her cheek.

Chapter Thirty-eight

The bus from Larache to Fez took over eight hours. It was a creaking old vehicle that lumbered slowly along the bumpy roads and stopped at nearly every village they passed. All the passengers seemed to have huge amounts of luggage that took ages to load or unload, and some of them even brought animals. It took nearly ten minutes for one man to coax his goat on board, then another ten minutes to get it off again a few kilometres down the road.

As they drove through the valley near Fez, Leila looked at the peaks and said, 'I'm glad there are mountains. They're not as high as the ones at home but still . . .'

As soon as they got off the bus they were surrounded by people offering themselves as guides. Leila chose one and told him where they wanted to go. He led them through an arch in the city ramparts and into a maze of crowded alleys.

There was a constant babble of noise from people jostling in the narrow space between the shops and stalls. Buyers and sellers shouted at each other over the din. Porters yelled warnings as they tried to clear a path for themselves or their mules. Fountains splashed and hammers beat on metal. The air was rich with the smell of animal dung and leather and baking bread and spices and frying food.

The alleys turned and twisted and by the time they stopped in front of a heavy door in the side of a building, Liam had lost all sense of direction. Leila paid the guide and pushed the door open. Wooden stairs led upwards and a large key lay on the bottom step. Leila picked up the key and locked the door behind them.

They climbed the stairs and came out on to a wooden balcony that ran round the four sides of an open courtyard. Above them was the blue sky and below them was an intricate blue and green tiled floor with a small fountain in the middle. The babble of the city sounded far away and the loudest noise was the splattering of the fountain.

They walked round the balcony past lattice doors until Leila pushed one open and showed Liam into a small room with a bed, a wooden table and a chair.

'It's like a monastery,' he said.

'It is in a way – people come here to study The Work. But it's been left empty for us. This is your room. I'll have the one next door.'

Leila walked to the door.

'Why?' Liam called as she was about to go out. 'Why has it been left for us?'

'Because we need somewhere to stay.'

'But how did they know we were coming? Why are we here?'

Leila looked at him and he thought she wasn't going to tell him but she came back and sat down next to him on the bed.

'They knew we were coming because . . . because this has all been planned, Liam. For years. Even before I knew about it. For years it has been planned that I would be in Fez in this week, in this month, in this year.'

'Why?'

'Because . . . in order for certain things to work . . . in order for them to be successful, they have to be done at a particular time in a particular place. And in this case, the place is Fez.'

'And the time is now?'

'Nearly now. We got here exactly on time – thanks to you. Any earlier or later would have been wrong. But now everything can mesh properly so that we can get the right result.'

'What do you mean – thanks to me? I didn't even know we had to be here at some special time.'

'Your head didn't know. But something else did. Just like it knew not to cross into Spain with André. Just like it knew to hide in the cave rather than go down to the river.'

'That was just luck.'

'It wasn't luck and you know it. Remember what you felt that morning in Port-Bou. You got a glimpse of it then. You almost saw it. It's the best part of you, the best part of all human beings. It's what's lying there inside, waiting to be woken up when people are ready for it. It's the next step in evolution. It's being in tune with other levels of existence that people can only guess at.'

She took his hand and lifted it to her lips and kissed it.

'You underestimate yourself, Liam. You don't realize what you're capable of. Most people don't.'

They spent the first two mornings exploring the intricate warren of alleyways and arches and little squares in the area around them. They always started off by trying to remember their route but they soon got distracted by the teeming life of the markets and stalls and workshops and took ages to find their way back.

They ate lunch at a noisy and crowded café across the way from their building then spent the afternoons in the peace and calm of the courtyard. The November sun was still hot and they sat in the shade, leaning against the ancient wooden wall. They talked about nothing and they talked about everything. They said things that made each other laugh. And they were quiet together. They sat so close that they could feel each other's heat where their shoulders touched, and they watched the water splashing in the fountain.

Then on the third day Leila said she wanted to find the way to a Medresa.

'A what?' Liam asked.

'A Medresa. It's a kind of school where people study the Koran. I know the name of this one but I don't know the way so we'll have to hire a guide.'

Leila asked the guide to walk slowly and Liam saw her noting the twists and turns they made during the twenty-minute journey. They stood outside the building while the guide pointed out the patterns carved in cedarwood above the doorway, then he led them inside. Ahead of them, at the end of the long dark hallway, was a huge, sunny courtyard where a fountain shot high into the air before falling back into a large pool. Suddenly Leila grabbed Liam's arm and stopped him.

'I don't want to go in!' she said urgently.

'Why?'

'I just don't.'

She turned round and hurried back on to the street. The guide followed them out and Leila paid him some money and said they didn't need him any more.

She looked pale and she was trembling.

'Are you OK?' Liam asked.

'I will be in a minute. Come on.'

She took his hand and they started on the way back. Her hand felt cold and she held on to him tightly. They walked fast and Liam was amazed when they turned a corner and he saw their building.

'Wow, we didn't get lost once!' he said. 'You're a genius.'

'That's me – a genius,' she joked, relaxing her grip on his hand.

They went to the café and sat outside, drinking mint tea and Leila was back to her usual self, pointing out things that interested or amused her about the passing crowds.

'I love it,' she said, looking out at all the bustle. 'All this energy. All this movement. Life's such an incredible thing.'

They ate a hot, spicy couscous for lunch and then Leila wanted to find the way out to the ramparts that surrounded the city. Then when they got there she decided that it would be fun to take a long walk in the hills outside. By the time they got back, Liam was exhausted. Even then she wasn't satisfied and she insisted on climbing the five flights of stairs to the top of the building.

It was worth the long climb though. They stood on the flat roof just as the sun was going down over the city. The honey-coloured walls of the ramparts, the white houses, the golden domes and minarets of the mosques and palaces, all were bathed in a blood-red light.

They stayed gazing over the city until it was dark.

Liam woke up in the middle of the night and heard someone walk along the balcony. He got out of bed quietly, eased the door, and looked out. Leila was walking down the stairs to the courtyard. She crossed the shadowy area and sat down, a pale figure, in the patch of silver light from the moon. She looked up at the sky for a long time, leaning back on her elbows, then she sat up straight and bowed her head. A stillness fell over her figure.

He moved forward softly and sat on the balcony, looking down at her through the wooden rails. She stayed motionless for over an hour then suddenly she stirred and stood up.

Liam darted back into his room and lay down on his bed. He heard her soft footsteps come up the stairs and stop outside his door.

'Can I come in?'

'Yes.'

The door swung open and then closed behind her.

She came to the side of his bed and sat down.

'Can I stay with you, Liam?'

'Yes.'

He moved over and she lay down beside him.

She put her head on his chest and he curved his arm protectively round her shoulder.

He couldn't hear or see her, but he knew she was crying by the warm tears that rolled off her cheek and soaked into his T-shirt just above his beating heart.

They lay like that until Liam saw the pale dawn begin to light up the holes in the lattice door. Then he fell asleep.

When he woke she had gone.

He got up and went out on to the balcony. He had just noticed that the sky was grey and a thin drizzle was falling on to the courtyard when he heard Leila come out of her room. She was carrying the travel bag. She put it down in front of him.

'I want you to do me a big favour, Liam. Will you promise to do it?'

'OK,' he said.

'I mean it – promise. You'll do whatever I want.'

'OK, I promise.'

She took a deep breath. 'I want you to go.'

'What?'

'I want you to leave me here and go back to England.'

His heart stopped and then started again with a burst of blood that made his knees feel weak.

'What?'

'You promised, Liam,' she said, taking hold of his hands. 'I want you to go to the British Consulate here in the city and give yourself up. They'll send you home. The police will question you about Doctor Prior but they'll soon realize that you're innocent. I want you to go back to school and take your exams. I want you to live your life.'

'Leila, don't muck around.'

'I'm not. I'm not.' She squeezed his hands and looked intently into his eyes. 'You got me here. And I could never have made it without you. But you've got to leave me. Your job's done. Please, Liam. If you care about me, just go.'

'No!'

'Please – you promised. This is so hard, don't make it worse. I know what you feel. And I feel the same. But you've got to let me go.'

'Go? Where? Where are you going?'

'Away. I've got no choice. It has to happen like this. It's part of the plan. It's more important than you and me. You've got to understand that.'

Her eyes burned into his.

'They'll put me in care!' he shouted but that wasn't what he wanted to say. He wanted to scream that he loved her.

She let go of his hands and bent down and picked up the travel bag. She leaned forward and her lips lightly touched his.

'You promised,' she said.

He took the bag from her and followed her down the stairs. She opened the door and he stepped out into the alley.

He turned but the door was closing. He saw her tear-filled eyes. Then she was gone.

He heard the key turn and the lock slide into place.

The thin rain swirled in the alley and fell on his head and shoulders.

Chapter Thirty-nine

Liam sat in the café and watched the door of the building. His heart was still racing and his face burned with the heat of the thoughts that whirled round his brain.

She'd sent him away.

Well, he wouldn't go. She'd tricked him into promising.

He had to honour the promise.

He couldn't keep the promise.

She would hate him for breaking it.

He couldn't keep it. He couldn't. There would be nothing for him. Alone. Without her.

But he'd promised.

Round and round, round and round, while his hands trembled too much to pick up the glass of mint tea on the table.

It was part of the plan. More important than him and her. No. Nothing was more important. He didn't believe in the plan. He couldn't be alone again.

But he'd promised.

The door opened and Leila came out. She was wearing the green caftan. The hood was up over her head. She closed the door and looked up and down the alley. But not over at the café.

She turned left under the archway and walked away down the hill. He picked up the bag and followed. He would go with her wherever she was going. He'd make her see that she still needed him.

The alleyways were crowded but he kept the green hood in sight among all the other bobbing heads. Whenever she turned left or right into another alley he had a flutter of panic until he reached the corner and saw the green hood still there ahead of him. Then suddenly he recognized where he was and he realized where she was going. The Medresa.

When he got to the end of the alley and out on to the square, Leila was already standing in front of the dark entrance hall of the Medresa. He stopped. She stood motionless for a few moments then took a couple of paces forward. She reached out and held on to the edge of the wooden doorway as if she felt unwell. Liam was just about to run over to help her when she straightened up and walked through into the darkness.

He forced himself to wait for a few seconds then he crossed the square. By the time he got to the entrance hall she was already out in the courtyard. He saw her stop by the fountain. She threw back the hood and glanced up at the sky as if she had only just noticed the drizzle. Then she walked away out of sight.

He hurried through the entrance hall to the edge of the courtyard. Leila was walking slowly towards a group of tourists who were listening to a guide who was pointing to a minaret that towered above the green tiled roof. She stopped and studied the tourists for a moment then turned away as if the person she was searching for wasn't there.

Behind her back, Liam saw someone step out from an archway in the far corner of the courtyard. It was a man wearing a dark-blue robe with a hood pulled low over his face. His arms were crossed in front of him so that his hands were hidden in the wide sleeves of the robe.

A jag of fear ran down Liam's neck.

Leila turned round as if she had sensed the man behind her. The man kept walking towards her. His right hand jerked out of the sleeve. He was holding a gun.

'Leila!' Liam screamed. 'Run!'

Leila glanced back at him in surprise.

'Stay there!' she shouted.

Then she turned back to the man and began walking towards him.

She raised her hands out to the side as if in surrender.

The man swept the hood away from his head. It was Nayeem.

Liam began to run.

Nayeem lifted the gun and fired.

Leila jerked backwards and staggered.

Liam was running. Running, with his arms held out as if he could catch her and break her fall.

He saw her hit the ground. But he kept running as the echo of the gunshot bounced round the walls and a woman began to scream.

Leila was lying on her side. He dropped to his knees and gently rolled her towards him then lifted her into his arms. There was a cut on her face and for an instant he thought she had only been grazed by the bullet. Then he felt her take a deep rattling breath and he looked down at her chest. Blood was welling out through the tattered hole in the green material of the caftan.

He looked away in horror and up at Nayeem who was standing with the gun still held out in front of him. His face was blank and his eyes were fixed as if he had been frozen at the instant after he had fired the gun.

There was a terrible gasp from Leila as she tried to catch her breath.

Liam looked down at her and he knew she was dying.

And he knew she had come here to die. And he had helped to bring her here.

There was a shout and a scuffling noise and he saw a couple of men grab Nayeem from behind. The gun clattered to the ground and slid away across the tiles. One of the men swung something and hit Nayeem on the side of the head. He buckled at the knees and fell to the floor.

He lay still but one of the men kicked him in the ribs. Nayeem jerked and groaned.

'No, don't do that!' Liam yelled as the man raised his foot again.

The man looked at him and lowered his foot.

Leila felt as if she was floating, rocking in a boat. She could hear Liam's voice but too far away to make out what he was saying.

Her head was growing heavy and moving backwards so slowly. Pressing backwards so slowly into Liam's arms. But as her head moved backwards, the pain in her chest grew worse. The movement was pulling the bullet hole open. She could feel the cold air round the edges.

Then the pain stopped and the cold was gone.

Her heart was pounding in her ear. But it wasn't her heart. Her heart had stopped. And in the silence she could hear another heart.

Her eyes opened and she saw grey. Then movement.

Liam looking down at her.

Beautiful face.

It was Liam's heart.

His heart beating. For her.

Her eyes closing now.

Darkness now.

Then out of the darkness came a different sort of light.

And in the light, another face.

Girl's face. Who?

Never seen before. But always there.

A bit like me. Same age.

Age.

Of course. Keeper of the Age.

Girl. Same age.

That's why.

They thought I . . . was Keeper . . .

I die . . .

And . . .
Keeper . . .
is . . .
safe.
Good.

Liam saw the exact moment that Leila died. There was a relaxing. And she had gone.

He would never see her again. Never talk to her. Never laugh with her. Never.

She had gone and a vast emptiness opened up inside him.

Chapter Forty

Leila was right.

The British Consul arranged for him to be flown home. The police were waiting for him when he got off the plane but, after two days of questioning and checking up on facts, they let him go.

They soon found out that Nayeem's fingerprints matched some bloody marks on Dr Prior's walls. Liam told them about the driver but he was never found.

After Nayeem's trial in Morocco for the killing of Leila he was flown to England and put on trial for the murder of Dr Prior. In both cases he pleaded guilty and refused to make any further statement.

The police asked Liam if he knew why Nayeem had killed Dr Prior and Leila. He said he didn't know.

Nayeem was flown back to Morocco to begin his prison sentence. Three weeks later he was discovered hanging in his cell.

Certain things haunted Liam.

Silly things he couldn't get out of his mind.

Her green caftan.

'It's a waste,' she'd said, knowing it would be ripped by a bullet and soaked with blood. But she had looked so beautiful in it.

The tears he'd seen in her eyes as she closed the door on him on that last morning.

The tiny pile of clothes the Moroccan police made him identify as hers. It was all she had. He asked to keep them but they wouldn't let him.

The way her blood had dried on his hands.

Silly things.

He was taken back to Beeches Hall. But he only stayed there for one night.

His new Case Worker was called Tony Froome. Tony told him there was no chance of going back to Frazergate School, of course.

'Anyway, that whole scheme of placing people in private schools collapsed. Stupid damn idea in the first place. It was local authorities trying to cut costs as usual. But I've got a really nice foster family lined up for you. Mr and Mrs Carpenter. You'll like them.'

Liam did like them. They were easy to get on with and they didn't complain when he spent most of his time in his own room. They had a ten-year-old son called Robin. He was football mad and played for his school team. Liam hadn't played for ages but he spent hours kicking the ball around and teaching him tricks. He enjoyed seeing Robin happy.

'The Carpenters say you're great with Robin,' Tony said. 'But they feel you're a bit . . . well, cool with them. You are happy with them, aren't you, Liam?'

'Yes. I like them.'

'Good.'

He didn't tell Tony that he was deliberately cool because he knew what Mr and Mrs Carpenter were thinking. They looked on him as part of their 'social duty'. They were proud that they gave up part of their house to someone who 'needed help'. They never said that, of course, but his intuition told him it was true. And he trusted his intuition.

They weren't bad reasons to foster him – on the contrary, they were good reasons and he admired them. But he knew that the Carpenters wanted affection from him when they didn't really have any to give back. He would always be their 'social duty'.

Tony said he could choose any school he wanted but he decided to go back to his old one. He knew most of the teachers and kids and it was easy to fit in. His old friend Paul wasn't there though; his family had moved to Scotland.

Tony wanted him to do an extra year to catch up but Liam insisted on taking his GCSE exams with everyone else. He only had five months to catch up but he worked even harder than he had at Frazergate and when the results came out he got the best grades of the year.

'That's amazing,' Tony said when he saw the results. 'Why did the exams mean so much to you?'

'Wanted to prove something, I suppose,' Liam said.

It wasn't true but he knew Tony would believe it because it was the kind of thing Tony believed. Liam didn't want to tell him the real reason. The promise was between him and Leila. She'd made him promise to leave her and go home and get his exams. He had broken the first part of the promise, he wasn't going to break the other part.

'Tony, I need your help.'

'Of course. What?'

'Two things. I want to go to a college where I can do A levels in one year.'

'Why?'

'Because if I work hard I can do them in that time. And then I want to go abroad.'

'Abroad? Hold on. You'll only be seventeen. Your Care Order is till eighteen.'

'Yeah, but that's the other thing. I want you to arrange for me to be adopted. I've written to some people in Spain and they'd like to adopt me.'

'Spain? That'll be a nightmare sorting out.'

'You've got a year to do it,' Liam grinned.

'Well, thank you!' Tony grinned back.

*

Tony got him into a college and he started A level courses in French, Spanish and Arabic. It was hard work, especially the Arabic, but he loved it. Apart from the football sessions with Robin and the occasional Saturday night out at clubs with some people from college, he did nothing but read, make lists of vocabulary, and listen to language tapes.

He knew he was improving week after week and he wished Leila could be there to see his progress.

On the first anniversary of Leila's death it was announced that an anonymous millionaire had set up The Leila Khan Trust to help homeless teenagers.

The project got a lot of coverage on TV and in the papers. One reporter even turned up at the Carpenters' house and wanted to interview Liam. He refused to say anything but that didn't stop an article about him appearing two days later.

It had an old photo of him and it went through all the stuff about Dr Prior and how he and Leila had gone to Morocco. Then at the end it described him as '. . . a reformed character who is now studying hard. Just the kind of success story that The Leila Khan Trust was set up to promote.'

At first he was angry but then he realized that it didn't matter. People would soon forget.

And they did.

People didn't forget The Leila Khan Trust though. It went on getting more publicity and helping more homeless teenagers. And Liam wondered whether it was all part of the plan.

He tried not to think too much about that. Whenever he remembered all the things that Leila had told him about plans and evolution and other dimensions he just felt confused and uncertain. Besides, he had other things to concentrate on. His work.

*

He passed his exams. Passed them so well that Tony said he ought to go to Spain for a long holiday and then come back and go to university.

'I don't think so. After all your hard work to get me there I think I'll stay in Spain.'

Tony *had* worked hard. All the complicated paperwork with his parents had taken nearly a year but at last Liam was officially the adopted son of Miguel and Antonia Garcia.

A week after the exam results came out, he said goodbye to the Carpenters. They said they were sad but that they were proud of what he'd done and they hoped they'd helped him. He said that they had and he promised to write regularly.

Tony saw him off at the station.

'I'm really grateful for everything, Tony,' Liam said. And he was.

'My pleasure. I'm hoping for a few free holidays over there, you know!'

His train ticket was all the way to Madrid and Tony had given him a list of all the times and connections. But as soon as he got to London Liam threw the list away. Instead of catching the train to Paris, he caught a bus to Nottingham.

He had told the Garcias what he was planning and they had agreed. He was going to take the same route he had taken with Leila.

He stayed two days in Nottingham and went to all the places he could think of, but there was no sign of The Rat. The squat had been demolished. No one knew what had happened to him. Liam hoped he was warm and safe in his own flat somewhere. But he doubted it.

He waited nearly all day at a truck stop on the A1 before he found a driver who was going to France. This time, though, there was no fear when he showed his passport to the officials at the Tunnel.

The driver would have taken him all the way to Paris but he chose to get out at Calais and take the train. He even ordered coffee and croissants in the station buffet as he waited for the train.

Ahmad's house had been completely rebuilt after the fire and he was working at his printing presses when Liam walked in. He embraced Liam and immediately closed up shop and led him upstairs. They spent the afternoon talking and Liam answered all his questions about Leila's last journey.

'We were privileged to have our lives touched by her,' Ahmad said.

'I know.'

Ahmad took him next door to see Karim and a feast was arranged for the evening. Karim's young son was sent off to spread the news. By the time Liam sat down as guest of honour that evening, there were over thirty people there. Karim's wife and some neighbours had prepared wonderful food but the atmosphere was subdued as the meal began. Then Ahmad clapped his hands and stood up.

'Leila would want us to remember her with joy,' he said. 'A song!'

Karim stood up and began singing. Someone started clapping in time and soon everyone joined in. A couple of young children began to dance and the whole atmosphere changed.

Liam relaxed and thought about the time he had danced here with Leila. He suddenly realized that he had been remembering her all wrong. He felt sad when he thought about her. But that wasn't what she was like. Even when she knew she was moving towards her death she had loved life and she had lived it with such intensity. And how she had loved to laugh. And how she had made him laugh.

It was a wonderful evening and he felt changed by it.

The next day he knocked at the elegant house just off the Champs-Elysées. André opened the door and led him inside.

The diplomat was in the library.

'Miguel rang me to tell me what you are doing,' he said. 'André will drive you to the border. But listen, my son, you are not trying to live in the past, I hope.'

'No, I'm freeing myself,' Liam said, although he had never thought about it like that before.

'Good. That is what must be done. And it is what she would have wanted for you.'

André followed the same route down the Rhône Valley then along past Montpellier and round the coast until they reached Cerbère.

'No boat this time,' André said as Liam got out just before the frontier.

'No. No need to hide,' Liam said. 'Goodbye – and thanks.'

He crossed the frontier on foot and then walked down the hill to Port-Bou.

He sat for a long time near the harbour at Port-Bou, remembering that extraordinary moment when the world had suddenly become ten times more real and powerful than usual. He tried to recall what it was like to feel so alive. But he couldn't. It was just a whisper of a memory.

Nor could he find the fish truck. He asked, but he was told that the driver had gone out of business.

Things changed.

It took him nearly three days to hitch down to Madrid but he finally made it and rang Miguel.

He sat on the steps of the same museum waiting for him.

He remembered what he and Leila had talked about when they were there. He had been so hostile, so scared by what she was saying. But what was it really? Just that people had extra senses hidden inside them. And when these senses developed they could do things that only sounded weird and special because they were new. He could go along with that. He believed it. Almost *knew* it was true.

Yes, but she'd also talked about the fact that some people couldn't do it. Wanting isn't enough, she had said. Supposing that was him?

Well, if it was him – tough luck. There wasn't much he could do about it.

When Miguel drove up, Liam suddenly felt awkward. This was his new father getting out of the car. What would it be like?

It was easy. Miguel smiled and shook his hand and squeezed his shoulder. And they got in the car. As easy as that.

It was even easier with Antonia. She came out of the castle door as they drew up. She didn't say anything. She just put her arms round him and pulled him close.

And he knew that it wasn't 'social duty'. He was being welcomed with love.

The following July, nearly three years after Leila's death, Liam was at home in Sepudillo. He had just finished guiding a party of tourists round the castle. It was nearly midday and there would be no more tourists until early evening so he decided to have lunch and then either do some more plastering or fill out the application form for Madrid University.

He was heading for the front door when he was stopped by one of the people who had been on the tour. An Indian man.

'Excuse me,' the man said. 'I am Leila Khan's father.'

Liam spent two weeks in Shimla with Leila's parents.

It was a wonderful time and he felt Leila's presence everywhere. He felt he knew the rooms of the small palace and the trees of the garden – she had described them so well.

It was a painful time too. So strange, to look at her parents and suddenly catch a glimpse of Leila – the way she smiled, or moved her head, or wrinkled her forehead when she was puzzled.

On the day before Liam left, Mr Khan drove him out to the cemetery to visit Leila's tomb. It was covered with flowers and Mr Khan told him that people had begun to visit the tomb as a site of pilgrimage.

'They guess at the sacrifice she made,' he said.

Liam nodded.

He knew that she had made a sacrifice. She had known she was going to die. She had known it was part of a plan to protect the Keeper of the Age. She had believed that it was worth it. She had given her life for something. Liam knew that much. But he still didn't understand.

He could ask her father. He must know. Or maybe he didn't. Perhaps the daughter had known more than the father. But he wasn't going to ask.

Leila had always spoken about 'need to know'. He didn't need to know. Leila had already given him so much. That was enough to be going on with.

All he knew was that he wouldn't stop searching. She had taught him to have an open mind. Now he would have to learn how to fill it.

She had told him that it was possible to break the brain's lazy habits and start to think in a new way. Now he would have to find out how to do it.

She had given him a glimpse of something outside his ordinary senses. Now he would have to find it for himself.

That evening he stood in the garden and watched the moon rise over the Himalayas.

And he felt Leila very close to him.

Hatchet

By Gary Paulsen

Brian opened his eyes and screamed.
For seconds, he did not know where he
was, only that the crash was still happening
and he was going to die. Then silence . . .

When Brian's plane crash-lands, he finds
himself alone in the Canadian wilderness.

As a city boy, he is not used to living rough.
But Brian knows he has a choice. Death –
or a fight for survival . . .

Age 12+   ISBN: 0 435 12508 7

Heinemann
New Windmills

Founding Editors: Anne and Ian Serraillier

Chinua Achebe Things Fall Apart
David Almond Skellig
Maya Angelou I Know Why the Caged Bird Sings
Margaret Atwood The Handmaid's Tale
Jane Austen Pride and Prejudice
J G Ballard Empire of the Sun
Stan Barstow Joby; A Kind of Loving
Nina Bawden Carrie's War; Devil by the Sea; Kept in the Dark; The Finding; Humbug
Lesley Beake A Cageful of Butterflies
Malorie Blackman Tell Me No Lies; Words Last Forever
Martin Booth Music on the Bamboo Radio
Ray Bradbury The Golden Apples of the Sun; The Illustrated Man
Betsy Byars The Midnight Fox; The Pinballs; The Not-Just-Anybody Family; The Eighteenth Emergency
Victor Canning The Runaways
Jane Leslie Conly Racso and the Rats of NIMH
Robert Cormier We All Fall Down
Roald Dahl Danny, The Champion of the World; The Wonderful Story of Henry Sugar; George's Marvellous Medicine; The BFG; The Witches; Boy; Going Solo; Matilda; My Year
Anita Desai The Village by the Sea
Charles Dickens A Christmas Carol; Great Expectations; Hard Times; Oliver Twist; A Charles Dickens Selection
Peter Dickinson Merlin Dreams
Berlie Doherty Granny was a Buffer Girl; Street Child
Roddy Doyle Paddy Clarke Ha Ha Ha
Anne Fine The Granny Project
Jamila Gavin The Wheel of Surya
Graham Greene The Third Man and The Fallen Idol; Brighton Rock
Thomas Hardy The Withered Arm and Other Wessex Tales
L P Hartley The Go-Between
Ernest Hemmingway The Old Man and the Sea; A Farewell to Arms
Frances Mary Hendry Chandra
Barry Hines A Kestrel For A Knave
Nigel Hinton Getting Free; Buddy; Buddy's Song; Out of the Darkness
Anne Holm I Am David

Janni Howker Badger on the Barge; The Nature of the Beast; Martin Farrell
Pete Johnson The Protectors
Jennifer Johnston Shadows on Our Skin
Geraldine Kaye Comfort Herself
Daniel Keyes Flowers for Algernon
Clive King Me and My Million
Dick King-Smith The Sheep-Pig
Elizabeth Laird Red Sky in the Morning; Kiss the Dust
D H Lawrence The Fox and The Virgin and the Gypsy; Selected Tales
George Layton The Swap
Harper Lee To Kill a Mockingbird
Julius Lester Basketball Game
C Day Lewis The Otterbury Incident
Joan Lingard Across the Barricades; The File on Fraulein Berg
Penelope Lively The Ghost of Thomas Kempe
Jack London The Call of the Wild; White Fang
Bernard MacLaverty Cal; The Best of Bernard Mac Laverty
Margaret Mahy The Haunting
Anthony Masters Wicked
James Vance Marshall Walkabout
Ian McEwan The Daydreamer; A Child in Time
Pat Moon The Spying Game
Michael Morpurgo My Friend Walter; The Wreck of the Zanzibar; The War of Jenkins' Ear; Why the Whales Came; Arthur, High King of Britain
Beverley Naidoo No Turning Back
Bill Naughton The Goalkeeper's Revenge
New Windmill A Charles Dickens Selection
New Windmill Book of Classic Short Stories
New Windmill Book of Fiction and Non-fiction: Taking Off!
New Windmill Book of Haunting Tales
New Windmill Book of Humorous Stories: Don't Make Me Laugh
New Windmill Book of Nineteenth Century Short Stories
New Windmill Book of Non-fiction: Get Real!
New Windmill Book of Non-fiction: Real Lives, Real Times
New Windmill Book of Scottish Short Stories
New Windmill Book of Short Stories: Fast and Curious
New Windmill Book of Short Stories: Tales with a Twist

How many have you read?